I0630549

THE BUFFALO TRAIN
A FARADAY NOVEL BOOK 5

ROBERT VAUGHAN

JAMES REASONER

WOLFPACK
PUBLISHING
— EST 2013 —

WOLFPACK
PUBLISHING
— EST 2013 —

Published in the United States by Wolfpack Publishing, Las Vegas

wolfpackpublishing.com

Paperback ISBN 978-1-64734-522-8
eBook ISBN 978-1-64734-521-1

THE BUFFALO TRAIN
A FARADAY NOVEL BOOK 5

Chapter 1

John Creed knew the idea was bad from the start. The small town of Glory was a den of thieves and killers, not to mention the Theron family.

One of whom was the reason Creed was about to ride into town, taking his life in his hands.

The young Texan was tall, with dark hair under a sweat-stained flat-brimmed hat. His blue shirt covered a lean frame wrapped in whipcord muscle. A Colt .44 with polished walnut grips rode easily in the holster attached to the gunbelt strapped around his hips. He was in his mid-twenties and had served with the 12th Texas Cavalry during the Civil War.

Once the war ended, he had drifted back to Texas, where he found nothing of his former life—a familiar story for many returning home from that conflict. So, without wasting any time since there was nothing there to hold him, he began making his way north through Indian Territory and into Kansas, working for numerous and varied employers until he found something he liked:

working as a guard on the railroad.

That job brought him into contact with a man called Matthew Faraday.

Faraday was the founder and owner of Faraday Security Service. A silver-haired, distinguished-looking gentleman, Faraday had a fondness of cigars and was as tough as whang leather despite his urbane appearance.

He also held a security contract with the major rail lines, which was how Creed had met him after foiling the robbery of a gold shipment single-handedly. That incident had led to Faraday offering Creed a job, and the young Texan, having nothing better to do, had accepted.

Lucky Theron was wanted for his part in an unrelated train robbery in Hollister, Nebraska that saw two guards shot, one of them fatally. Theron had lived up to his nickname when he was the only one of the five outlaws to escape the carnage that occurred while they were trying to liberate a pay shipment from the Union Pacific's Eastern Express. Unfortunately, during the melee, he had been recognized.

While that was going on, John Creed was delivering a prisoner to Van Buren, Arkansas. He had received a wire there from Matthew Faraday, giving him the job of capturing Lucky Theron and returning him to face justice.

Unless, of course, Theron put up too much of a fight.

If that happened, Creed was supposed to bring him back dead.

He stopped the buckskin in the shade of a tall hickory tree and studied the town before him from the rise in the trail. Thin wisps of woodsmoke rose lazily into the cool mountain air, the only stains on an otherwise-clear azure sky.

Reaching up to his shirt, Creed took off his Faraday Security Agency badge and tucked it into his right boot. Riding in there with that on display would likely earn him an ounce of lead, probably in the back, and a long sleep in a six-foot-deep hole.

As far as he was aware, Lucky had at least two brothers, and both parents still alive. Then there were numerous cousins and uncles and aunts. As far as law went, he had been warned to expect almost anything.

"Let's go see what we have in there, horse," Creed said as he eased the animal forward.

* * *

The town had a peculiar and particularly unpleasant odor about it, akin to death and manure. He wasn't quite sure which was which, but it was all mixed in there.

The buckskin splashed through a muddy puddle, the remnants of the heavy rain the day before. Along the main street, most of the buildings were of log construction, with very few false-fronts or frame buildings.

A sudden thought crossed the Texan's mind as he continued along the rutted and muddy road; these people didn't get many visitors to their stinking

Colorado town. He could tell from the way they watched him with a mixture of keen interest and hostility as he passed.

Creed drew level with a saloon that had a crude hand-painted sign out front that read *Theron's House*. He turned the animal toward the hitch rail. It drew up at the crossbeam and stood waiting for its rider to dismount. Creed climbed down, saddle leather creaking with his movements. Reaching for his Winchester Yellow Boy in its scabbard, he looped the reins over the rail, then began climbing the steps onto the deteriorated plank boardwalk. The rifle had a full load of .44 Henry cartridges in its magazine.

"Going somewhere, mister?" a voice said from his left.

Creed stopped and turned to face the speaker, a thin-faced man, unshaven, with narrow shoulders and hips. His oily and straggly hair and his clothes appeared as if they hadn't been washed for a week or two.

"I thought I might get myself a drink."

"Where you from?"

"What's that got to do with you?"

The man opened his coat to reveal a badge. "That's what it's got to do with me. The name's Jack Theron, town marshal."

"Creed."

"You're from Creede, Colorado? What you doin' up here?"

A faint smile touched Creed's lips. "That's my name, not where I'm from."

"Oh. Creed who?"

4

"Just Creed."

"Well, Just Creed," Jack Theron growled, "what the hell are you doin' in Glory?"

"Just passing through."

The marshal squinted at him suspiciously and said, "I'll be keeping an eye on you. You cause any trouble, and you'll face the full force of Glory law."

As if to get his point across, Jack Theron turned his head and looked along the street. Creed followed his gaze and saw a large cottonwood at the end of the street. For a moment, he wondered what the lawman was looking at.

Then he saw it. Hanging from a thick horizontal branch was a rope with a noose at the end of it.

Creed nodded. "I understand."

"I'm glad you do," Jack said, giving him a gap-toothed smile.

"Can I go now?"

"Sure."

Creed turned away from the marshal and pushed his way through the batwing doors into the saloon. The interior was gloomy, a couple of lanterns, which threw no more light than candles, the only illumination. It smelled of unwashed bodies, smoke, and stale beer. The bar was typical of many saloons he'd been in, consisting of a couple of planks set up on barrels. The numerous rough-hewn tables were crowded together, which made getting through next to impossible when all the chairs were full.

"Buy a lady a drink, stranger?" a husky voice purred over his shoulder.

Creed turned to face a woman standing no more

than four feet from him. The bodice of her low-cut, torn, grimy red dress barely covered large breasts that strained over the top of it. As he took in the sight of her, she smiled, revealing broken, tobacco-stained teeth, and a shiver ran up his spine.

"I can curl your toes, too. You just give me a try and see."

Creed shook his head. He was enough of a gentleman to keep a look of revulsion off his face as he said, "No, thanks."

She pouted. "You sure?"

He nodded. "Maybe another time."

Creed walked up to the bar and placed a coin on the counter. He looked at the fat barkeep and said, "Whiskey."

The man picked up a bottle from a shelf behind him and poured some of the dark liquid into a dusty glass. As he took the coin, he said, "Wise choice you made there, stranger."

The glass stopped halfway to Creed's lips. "What? The whiskey or the woman?"

"That's Lucky's special girl. He don't like strangers messing with her."

"I take it she doesn't make much money?"

"Only what Lucky gives her."

Creed nodded. "How often does he come in?"

"Every afternoon about four," the bartender said. He dug into his pocket for a pocket watch and opened it. "Thirty minutes from now."

"I see," Creed said. "What about the other girls?"

"There ain't any others." The man made a face. "This, ah, ain't a very big town. Not enough customers to support much trade if you know what I mean."

Creed drank his whiskey and motioned for the bartender to pour him another. "Does she know she's his special girl?"

"Sure, she does."

"So, her wanting me to buy her a drink was just to make Lucky jealous?"

"That's right. We don't get many strangers through here. The last one she did it to took her up on her offer." The man grimaced. "Don't know why. I've seen a better face on the rear end of a mule."

Creed felt a little bad about it, but he had to chuckle. "What happened to him?"

"Lucky shot him, and Clarissa cackled like a hen laying eggs as she watched."

Creed drank the second glass and bought a third. "This stuff tastes like horse piss."

The bartender nodded. "Try complaining to the owner."

"Who is the owner?"

"Tyrone Theron. Lucky's brother."

"Good Lord, the place is loaded with them. That marshal I met outside, he was a Theron, too."

"Mister, the place is riddled with them and their kin."

"If I was to get into trouble in this town, how would I get out of here in a hurry?" Creed asked.

"If I was you, I'd leave now before that happens."

"Maybe you're right," Creed said.

But the bartender wasn't looking at him anymore. Instead, he was looking over Creed's shoulder at the doorway. "When it rains, it pours," he muttered.

Turning to look, Creed saw a handsome, dark-haired man with a thin mustache standing just inside the room, glancing around. He muttered under his breath when the man saw him and started toward the bar. Pulling up in the vacant space beside Creed, the man said, "I'll have a beer, barkeep."

"Don't have beer."

"Tequila?"

"Uh-huh." He grunted and walked along the bar to get a bottle.

"What are you doing here?" Creed asked the man.

"Faraday didn't think you'd follow orders and not come in on your own. Looks like he was right. He sent me along to pull your butt out of any trouble you might get yourself into."

A tall, broad-shouldered hombre, Hector Yates was another man out of the agency. On his right hip, he wore a Remington .44-caliber.

"I don't need any help," Creed whispered.

"No? How do you think you're going to get Lucky out of here on your own?"

Creed remained silent.

"Didn't think so."

The barkeep returned with a bottle of tequila and poured a drink. Yates paid him and then drank. Creed waited until the bartender walked back along the bar before he said, "I have an idea, but it's going to take both of us to pull it off."

"Why do I get the feeling I'm not going to like it?"

Creed smiled. "Come on, Yates. What could go wrong?"

* * *

"You still up for that drink, or do you want to do something a little more special?" Creed asked Clarissa after he'd ambled over to the table where she sat.

Her smile was mischievous as she stood up, and her eyes sparkled because she knew what would happen and was excited by the prospect.

"You want to skip the drink and just on to my room for a poke?"

"Why not?" Creed said. "I already had a drink anyway."

"Well then, handsome, let's get to it."

She led him toward the back of the saloon and out through a rear door to a small room with a bed in it. Creed, however, had no intention of even taking his hat off. By the time Clarissa realized that, it was too late.

* * *

"That stranger is digging his own grave," the bartender said to Yates.

"What do you mean?"

"When Lucky finds out he's out there with his girl, he's going to shoot him. Or worse."

"I'd hate to be in his shoes, then," Yates said with a shake of his head.

"You and me both. I almost feel sorry for him."

Yates went back to his drink, biding his time, and waited for events to unfold.

It didn't take long. The doorway went dark as

a large figure filled the void, and a man befitting of the shadow he threw entered the bar. Stopping momentarily, he looked around, his scarred face going from passive to suspicious. He fixed his gaze on the bartender and rumbled, "Where is she, Vern?"

The barkeep's expression was that of a man expecting to be shot for telling him the truth. "Who's that, Lucky?" he choked out, feigning ignorance.

"You know who, damn it. She better not be with the stranger whose horse I seen outside at the hitch rail." As he finished his sentence, Lucky Theron adjusted the gunbelt around his waist. "Damn it, Vern, I'm waiting."

"She's out the back, Lucky," Vern squeaked.

"Son of a—" Lucky snarled and lumbered toward the rear door.

Vern edged closer to Yates and said, "He's the biggest man I ever saw."

"He's the biggest anything I ever saw," the Faraday agent countered.

The outlaw grasped the doorknob and flung the door wide, almost ripping it off its hinges. He took a step through and then suddenly reappeared, staggering backward, arms windmilling wildly.

Yates heard the barkeep gasp as Creed charged into the saloon, fists cocked and a look of grim determination on his face. He closed on the big outlaw and shot two more blows to the killer's body, which caused him to drop his arms to protect his middle.

That was what Creed wanted him to do because it left his scarred face unguarded. Creed changed his target and landed another blow on Lucky's jaw.

The big man went down, his fall splintering a table that had just been vacated by a couple of drinkers. The outlaw shook his head and began to rise. So far, all was going according to plan, but as Yates watched, he had an inkling that was about to change.

A shrill cry sounded over the din. *"Kill the son of a bitch, Lucky!"*

Yates glanced at the open doorway to the back room and saw Clarissa standing there.

With a loud roar, Lucky charged Creed, and his shoulder hit the agent in the middle and drove him toward the bar. When they connected, the impact knocked the boards aside and overturned one of the empty barrels. The two men kept going. The wall behind the bar, on the other hand, was a more solid obstacle.

The whole saloon shuddered from the violent impact, and the bottles on the shelves crashed to the floor as the structures gave way. Creed let out a pained cry and started to pound on the outlaw's back. Lucky reared up and threw a wild punch at the agent's contorted face. At the last moment, Creed saw it coming and moved his head out of the way.

Once more the wall shook, and Lucky reeled away, cursing the pain that burned through his fist. Creed glanced at Yates.

"A little help, *amigo?*"

Yates smiled and drawled, "I thought you were doing pretty well on your own."

The expression on Yates's face changed when he saw Clarissa come up behind Creed with a raised chair. He moved to intervene, taking a few swift steps and grasping the chair before she could bring it down on the back of Creed's head.

"Weren't you ever told you should keep out of men's business?" he scolded her.

She let go of the chair and turned to face him, anger etched deep in her face. "Why, you lily-livered, pox-ridden, polecat-humping—"

"Uh-uh," he said, clamping a hand over her mouth. "Talk like that's not very ladylike."

He dropped the chair and forced Clarissa to sit down on it. "Stay right there and watch your man. Maybe even cheer him on a bit." He turned away from her, and a new string of profanity spewed from her lips. Yates shook his head. "No wonder you ain't married yet. Mouth on you like an outhouse."

"You son—" The rest was drowned out by the loud crash of Creed falling through a table, turning the once-solid piece of furniture into kindling.

Lucky had gathered himself and was now counterattacking like a one-man Confederate regiment at Shiloh. He leaned down, picked Creed up by his collar, and heaved him across the room. For a moment, the agent felt what it was like to be a bird, one without wings, as he crashed to the floor. The air rushed from his lungs.

Gasping to get his breath, Creed looked up to see the bear of a man coming toward him. For a moment, he contemplated drawing his Colt and shooting the outlaw. That would save a whole world of hurt and pain. However, by the time his addled mind was made up, Lucky was dragging him to his feet once more.

Lucky held him erect so he could stare into Creed's eyes. "Who the hell are you?"

Creed blinked to focus. "I'm your pappy."

With a roar, the outlaw carried him toward the entrance and threw him across the threshold. Creed once more did his best impression of a limp-winged buzzard before he crashed onto the street. Rolling over, he moaned, coughed, and tried to drag his knees up beneath him to stand.

The small crowd from inside followed Lucky out into the bright sunlight that bathed Glory. Creed held up a hand and spat blood into the dust. In a thick voice, he said, "OK, friend, you win."

"The hell you say," the outlaw growled. "I ain't won anything yet. I'm just gettin' started."

Creed winced. "You sure? Don't much feel like it from where I am."

"I'm going to kill you, stranger. Bit by bit."

Creed managed to climb to his feet. "Somehow, I was afraid of that."

"What the hell is going on here?" Jack Theron roared as he approached the two combatants.

"The stranger was with my girl," Lucky growled.

"Damn it, Lucky, Clarissa is a damned whore."

"I don't care. She's *my* whore."

"He wasn't with me," the woman shouted. Yates had let her out of the chair, and she had rushed out to the boardwalk. "He was waiting for Lucky. I bet the son of a bitch is a bounty hunter."

Just like that, the situation went from bad to worse.

Everyone stopped. Heads turned, and gazes hardened. Creed's heart sank since he knew the only solution involved bloodshed, and there was a good chance some of it would be his.

Should have listened to that bartender's advice, Creed, old son.

"Are you sure?" Lucky asked.

"Why else would he lay in wait for you? He sure wasn't trying to get frisky with me."

The outlaw turned his gaze back to Creed. "Is she right, stranger? You a stinking bounty hunter?"

Creed shook his head. "Nope. I ain't a bounty hunter." The agent glanced around the hostile crowd, looking for Yates. His gaze came back to Lucky. He shrugged. "Your girl is lying."

"What? Why would I lie?" Clarissa yelled.

"Yeah, why would she lie?" Lucky demanded.

"Because I tricked her into the room and couldn't pay. Besides, she's a mite, you know, ugly."

"I'd believe that," a voice called.

Lucky turned and said, "Shut up, Tyrone."

The man who had spoken from his place on the boardwalk wore a black suit and a fancy vest over a white shirt. A black hat was canted at a jaunty angle on his head, and he had a black cheroot clamped between his teeth. He grinned around it at his brother Lucky.

"You hear that, Lucky?" Clarissa screeched. "The bastard called me ugly. Shoot him!"

"Hold it!" Jack called. He stepped between Creed and Lucky and said to Creed, "Mister, you're comin' with me."

"Where?"

"Jail. I'm going to lock you up there for the night,

and then tomorrow you can go before the town council. They can decide what to do with you."

Creed's relief must have been obvious because the marshal went on, "Don't look so thankful. The last six men—actually, everyone who goes before the town council—ends up on Cottonwood Hill."

"What's Cottonwood Hill?" Creed asked, even though he was afraid he already knew the answer to that question.

What he didn't know was where in blazes Hector Yates had gotten off to or what the other agent was doing.

"It's where we bury our dead," the marshal told him.

"Just let me kill him, Jack!" Lucky snapped. "It'll save all the bother."

"Your pa won't be happy with that, Lucky. You know what he's like."

"Damn it!"

"All right, stranger," the lawman said. "Turn around."

Under the circumstances, Creed didn't have much choice in the matter. He did as he was ordered, and Jack stepped behind him and took the Colt from its holster. Then he jammed the barrel of his weapon into the agent's back hard enough to make him wince. "Now, start walking."

* * *

"Wait there," Jack growled as he walked around Creed. He reached up to a peg on the wall and took down the key for the single cell at the back of the room.

"Why does he get so upset over someone—" Creed stopped.

"Someone what?"

"Well, she's not the best-looking apple in the box. Matter of fact, I've seen horses' rear ends looked more inviting than her."

Jack gave him a wry smile. "She is a tad ugly, ain't she?"

"A tad? You're a kind man, Jack Theron."

The smile vanished. Jack gave a curt nod toward the cell and said, "In there."

"You're really going to lock me up for trying to poke a whore?" Creed asked.

"That's exactly what I intend to do."

"So, you'll condemn a man to death for doing what comes naturally?"

"The council will decide your fate," Jack reaffirmed.

The door behind them opened, and Hector Yates walked in. Jack glanced at the newcomer, then said, "I'll be with you in a minute." He turned back to Creed. "In the cell."

Creed looked over Jack's shoulder and saw Yates's shoulder dip. His hand rose with the Remington in his fist, and it crashed down on the back of the town marshal's head. The man dropped like a pole-axed steer.

Yates looked at Creed and asked, "How's that plan of yours working out?"

"Just fine." Creed was too stubborn to admit

otherwise.

"Well, what now?"

"Let's get our friend here into the cell and tie him up."

They worked quickly. When they were finished, Yates stared at Creed, waiting for him to enlighten him as to his next move.

That decision was taken out of their hands when the door opened and Lucky Theron entered the jail. "Jack, I'm not taking any more of your crap. I want that—" He froze, and his jaw dropped open. "What the hell?"

"Keep coming, Goliath," Yates snapped. "Close the door behind you."

"You won't get away with this!"

Creed drew his Colt, which he'd retrieved from Jack before locking him up. He said to Yates, "Get the horses."

"What about him?"

"Steal one."

The agent shrugged. "Makes sense, I guess."

Yates went outside. Creed said to Lucky, "Sit in the chair."

The big outlaw sat, a scowl on his face. "Who the hell are you, anyway?"

"I'm a Faraday detective."

"A what?"

"Never mind."

Creed seated himself on the edge of the desk and waited for Yates to return. A half-hour of tedious monotony passed before the other agent reappeared.

"The horses are around the back," Yates reported. "The sun is still up, so we're going to be riding out of town in broad daylight."

Creed thought for a moment, scratching his head. "We'll have to wait for dark. Keep an eye out the back just in case someone finds the horses. I'll watch the front. Just be ready to get the hell out of here."

"You're all gonna die," Lucky growled.

"If I were you, Lucky, I'd be more worried about other things."

"What are you talking about?" The outlaw looked confused.

"If you've been cavorting with that whore of yours, I wouldn't be surprised to see a certain portion of your anatomy wither and drop off."

The big man had to think about that for a few seconds, frowning as if his head hurt. When understanding dawned in his eyes, he snarled and lunged forward, coming up out of the chair.

The Colt in Creed's hand swept around in a backhanded arc and caught the outlaw across the bridge of his nose. Crimson blood spurted and Lucky slumped, stunned but not quite out of it.

"I owe you a few more of those," Creed said. "Keep it up, and I'll deliver them all."

"You broke my nose," Lucky wailed, cringing with pain.

"I guess that makes you not that lucky after all."

* * *

18

It was an hour after the sun went down. The pair's luck had held, and they hadn't been discovered. Now it was time to leave.

"Get up," Creed ordered Lucky.

The outlaw climbed to his feet, battered but still defiant. "You won't get out of Glory alive."

"Let's see, shall we?" The retort was almost nonchalant.

He escorted the outlaw out the back, where Lucky climbed aboard a sturdy-looking bay mare. The two agents swung into their saddles, and they all rode down a narrow alley toward the street. Creed looked around when they reached the alley's mouth. The street appeared to be deserted.

"All right, let's go."

They emerged from the darkness and turned left onto the street. The sound of the horses' hoofbeats seemed unbelievably loud as they rode along. As they passed the saloon, they could hear raucous noise coming from within. The batwings swung open, and a man staggered out onto the boardwalk. He stared briefly at the riders before stumbling to the edge of the walk, bending over double, and hurling the contents of his stomach onto the street.

Creed grimaced at the sight and smell but felt a sense of relief wash over him. Then the man straightened up and stared at them again.

"Hey, Lucky, where you going?" he called.

"Tell him to mind his own business," Creed said out of the corner of his mouth.

"Lucky, where you going?" the drunk repeated.

Lucky's voice exploded from his throat. "They're

the law! Get the boys!"

"Damn it," Yates said and drew his Remington, snapping off a hasty shot at the drunk but missing. The man yelped and threw himself back into the safety of the saloon.

Creed slapped the rump of the horse Lucky was riding, and the animal lunged forward and broke into a run. Creed and Yates dug their heels into the flanks of their own mounts. Without looking back, they could hear men tumbling out of the saloon. Gunshots roared and echoed from the buildings.

By the time the riders reached the edge of town, the shooting behind them had stopped. Creed guessed the men were trying to organize themselves to come after them, and he began considering their options. A mile out of Glory, Creed eased his horse to a halt.

Yates pulled his mount up beside him and asked, "What are we stopping for?"

"Twenty miles to the north of here, the UP Line runs between Omaha and Cheyenne. A mail and freight train passes through most nights, heading east not long after midnight. We should be able to make it and flag them down."

"What are we waiting here for?" Yates asked. "Lead the way."

Chapter 2

There were four of them. Four men riding in the moonlight, leading a cow—a cow that acted more like a damned mule than a bovine. The lead rider turned in his saddle and whispered harshly, "Will you hurry the hell up?"

"Dang it, Rio, I'm doing the best I can with this thing. Unless you want to take over?"

Rio Wade glared through the darkness, and although the rider known as Slim couldn't see Wade's eyes, he could feel the heated gaze burning into his hide.

"You were saying, Slim?" Wade asked, his voice holding a hard edge.

Wade hailed from Missouri. He'd served in the war with the 1st Missouri Cavalry, and when it was over, he'd moved to Kansas, where he'd found work with a man named Hank Miles. The men with him, like many others, had also fought.

He was a solidly built man with a scar on his cheek, courtesy of a Rebel saber. His eyes were dark and brooding, and his attire was totally black like that of a man in constant mourning for a loved one.

From the shadows ahead of them appeared another rider. Wade drew his horse to a halt and dropped his hand to the Colt Navy on his hip. He was about to pull it clear of leather, but he stopped when he heard a voice call, "It's me, Rio."

"Damn it, Kent, I almost shot you."

"Good thing you didn't," the man replied. "The herd is bedded down just over that ridge a mile ahead."

Wade gave a satisfied nod. "All right. Kent and I will take the cow with us. The rest of you wait here just in case we have trouble. If there is, come running, and we'll stampede the herd. Otherwise, you wait and go nowhere."

Slim led the cow forward. "Here, Rio. I think I'm getting sick from this blasted thing."

"You're a damned idiot," Wade growled, snatching the rope out of the man's hand.

He kneed his horse forward, following Kent, and they crested the rise, coming to a stop below the ridge on the other side so they wouldn't be skylined.

Kent said, "There are riders on all four sides of the herd. If we let the animal go here, it'll wander on down to get to the water because it ain't had none for a couple of days."

"All right," Wade said and dismounted. He untied the rope attached to the cow and let it go. As expected, the beast started down the slope toward the lowing herd and the water it desired.

"Now all we have to do is wait until they reach the river and let the boss do what he wants."

* * *

"Breakaway!" The shout rang out as a brindle-colored Longhorn decided to split from the rest of the herd on the right.

Upon hearing the call, a flank rider kicked his Texas cow pony hard, and the animal leaped into a run and dashed after the cow. The rider urged the horse on, and from his position on the low ridge Max Kelly, the trail boss, watched the display with pride. The steer hadn't gone far when the smart little horse headed it off and turned it back toward the strung-out herd. He grunted and turned his head toward the horizon, his gray eyes scanning the ground ahead. Up there somewhere was their next river crossing— the Canadian, their last one before they were out of Indian Territory, and one river closer to the new railhead at Abilene.

They'd already come a long way but still had a distance to go. They'd crossed the Red River with almost two thousand head of Longhorns, fifteen hands, and sixty horses. Along the way, they'd lost a few head of cattle, five horses to Indians, and two men. The stock loss wasn't bad considering. However, whenever he lost a man, Kelly took it personally.

He took off his battered hat, revealing a head of mostly gray hair. His face was weathered to walnut brown, and his whiskers were getting longer by the day. Standing up in the stirrups, he stretched out the kinks in his back before dropping his rump back into his saddle. Kelly winced as he settled back down.

The sound of hoofbeats drew his attention, and he

turned to see the approach of the flank rider who'd caught the runaway steer. The rider reined in and took off a stained hat to reveal long dark hair that tumbled past small shoulders.

"We're going to have to shoot that animal, Pa," Eliza Kelly told her father. "It's more damn trouble than it's worth."

Kelly shook his head. "We need every head, Liza. You know that."

Kelly's daughter had grown up in the saddle. He swore she was better than any son he could have wished for. She could rope, brand, and break a horse as well as any man he knew, and by God, she could drive cattle.

Beneath the trail dust hid a pretty young woman whose resemblance to her mother was uncanny. Looks were as far as the similarities went to her elegant and graceful mother, who had passed on some time ago. Eliza was the ultimate tomboy. Put a dress on her, and it would be torn and filthy before an hour had passed.

"I still think the reverend could make a good stew from the bastard," she growled.

"Liza," he admonished her.

She rolled her eyes. "You get what you raise, Pa, and you raised a cowhand."

"It doesn't mean you have to cuss like one," he reminded her.

She rolled her eyes again. "Sh—"

"Liza! If your mother could hear you now."

She pulled her hair up and crammed her hat onto her head, then wheeled her horse and headed back toward the herd. Kelly watched her until she'd taken up her position, then turned his own horse and rode toward the head of the herd.

A mile farther along the Chisholm Trail, the Canadian River came into view. The cattle smelled the water ahead and quickened their pace. The point riders did their best to keep them contained, but the animals were thirsty, so Kelly shouted to his riders, "Let them go. They'll stop when they reach the river."

As Kelly drew closer to the river, many of the cows were already drinking their fill. He frowned when he saw a number of riders sitting and watching from the far bank. He stopped his horse on the southern bank and called, "Howdy, gents."

One of the men called back gruffly, "Are you Kelly with the Rafter K herd from Texas?"

The trail boss nodded. "I am. Who are you?"

"Hank Miles," the man replied. "We're here to look over your herd. Make sure there are no sick cattle amongst them."

"There are no sick cows in my herd," Kelly said.

"Then you won't mind if we look," Miles shot back.

A horse pulled up beside Kelly. "What's going on, Pa?" Liza asked.

"Damned jayhawkers, I suspect. They want to look over our herd to see if any of them are sick."

"Well?" Miles called.

"I already told you my answer."

The men on the opposite bank began to spread out. A quick count revealed there to be at least twenty of them. As one, they drew their guns and waited for the standoff to play out.

"The only way you get across that river is to let us look over your herd, Kelly. I'll give you until morning to decide. Until then, you stay on that side of the river."

"What if I just push my beeves across anyway, Miles?" Kelly said.

"We'll start shooting them as soon as they hit the bank on this side. Riders, too. We'll not have Texas Fever north of this line."

"Do you think he means it, Pa?" Liza asked her father.

"I don't know. Have the rest of the hands hold them here and take two others with you to look at the herd."

"You figure some might be sick?"

"No, I'm just making sure they ain't."

* * *

Hank Miles stared across the river at the trail boss. The bay beneath him moved gently before settling down.

Even in the saddle, Miles gave an impression of size and power. He had a barrel chest and shoulders like a bull. He wore a brown tweed suit, and a cream-colored hat rode on his bald head. The man's flinty stare was unwavering, his square jaw set firm.

Beside him, Rio Wade asked, "What do you figure he'll do?"

Miles shrugged. "I'll guess we'll find out come morning. Post three men on the river at all times to make sure they don't try anything."

26

"Mr. Miles," a short, stocky man on the opposite side began. "Maybe this is a bad idea. Maybe—"

"Shut up, Crown," Miles snapped at the cattle inspector. "You took my money. Now you see it through."

The man nodded nervously. "Yes, sir."

"I want McCoy's new town to fail. The longer it survives, the more drives are taken away from Ellsworth. And the more money I lose."

That was the crux of the matter. Apart from being a wealthy business owner, Miles was also a cattle trader. He offered the Texas trail bosses ten dollars a head less than the selling price and then sold them for the full price to the buyers back east, but to do that, the herds had to keep coming to Ellsworth.

Joseph McCoy had jeopardized the Ellsworth cattle trade by opening Abilene as a new railhead, a closer destination for the Texas herds, complete with yards. He'd lobbied the Kansas Pacific for a switch and sidings so this would be possible, and they'd obliged.

McCoy's final requirement was met when the Hannibal and St. Joseph Railroad agreed to ship the cattle to the slaughter yards in Chicago.

Recently though, the rumor of Texas Fever had been circulating. If anything was going to kill the Abilene trade, it would be a good dose of that. Miles' plan would help in two ways. First, it would stop the buyers from coming to Abilene to buy cattle. No buyers, no Abilene. Second, it gave control of the cattle market back to Miles in Ellsworth, where he could set the prices without fear of competition.

This herd across the river was the key to his plan working. The cow they had released into the herd the previous night would be the catalyst. There was nothing like a diseased herd and the death of two thousand Longhorns to upset everything.

"What now, boss?" Wade asked.

"We wait."

* * *

"Mr. Kelly, we've got a problem," Ben Pullen, the ramrod, told his boss. "You ain't gonna like it."

The man had a worried expression on his bearded face that portended bad news, and Kelly shook his head. "Tell me, Ben."

"We found a sick cow in the herd."

Kelly's face remained stoic. "What's wrong with it?"

"We don't know, but that ain't gonna matter to them fellas over the other side of the river. All they'll see is a sick cow and..."

He left the rest unsaid.

"Let's go and have a look at it."

Pullen led his boss to where the cow was set aside from the rest of the herd. He took one look at it and shook his head. The animal was skinny, its coat was dull, and it had snot running from its nose. The trail boss groaned.

"We could take it off somewhere and shoot it," Pullen suggested.

Kelly nodded. "Do it. Then burn it."

The sound of a horse loping up to them drew his attention, and Kelly looked around to see his daughter. She reined in, took one look at the cow, and asked, "Where did that come from?"

"Ben found it," Kelly said.

"But where did it come from?" she persisted.

Kelly looked at Liza. "I told you, Ben found it."

"It ain't one of ours."

The trail boss stared hard at his daughter. "What?"

"It ain't one of ours, Pa. It don't belong with this herd."

"Are you sure?"

"Sure, I'm sure. Look at the brand."

Kelly climbed down off his horse and walked over to the animal to see the brand better. It was the same as their brand, albeit a little rough around the edges. Liza said, "Someone did that with a running iron. I'd swear that on Ma's grave. And one more thing, I ain't seen it before now."

"You could be mistaken, Miss Liza," Pullen suggested tentatively.

She glared at him. "I been riding alongside these cows since we left Texas, Ben. I think I know by now what they all look like. I'm telling you this ain't one of ours."

"Then where did it come from?" Pullen asked.

Kelly looked toward the river. "It seems awful convenient that Miles and them riders show up and want to look at our herd right when this sick animal appears."

"You think they had something to do with it?" Pullen asked.

"I don't know, but take this animal somewhere away from here and shoot it. Make sure it won't be found. You've got until morning. Take Hawk and Teddy with you."

Pullen nodded. "Yes, sir."

Once the others were gone, Liza looked at her father. "What's going on, Pa?"

He shook his head, a worried expression on his face. "I'm damned if I know."

* * *

The following day broke warm under a clear blue sky. The cattle lowed mournfully while the hands rode around them, trying to keep them from wandering. On the opposite side of the river, three riders stood guard over the crossing. Woodsmoke from a campfire rose into the air, the thin tendril leaving a slight smudge over their camp.

The Rafter K crew had taken shifts to eat their breakfast, and only Kelly, the cook, and Liza were left in the camp. The trail boss came to his feet and walked over to the chuckwagon. He handed his plate over and said, "Reverend, once you're done here, I want you to start handing out the rifles. I'll send the men in a couple at a time."

"You might as well give me mine now," Liza said.

Kelly stared at his daughter.

"What?" she asked.

"You'd do well to stay out of this, girl," he stated.

"This herd is as much mine as it is yours, Pa. If there's fighting to be done, you have to count me in."

Kelly shook his head. He knew the look she was giving him. "Reverend, give me two of the rifles and some shells."

The old cook nodded. "Yes, sir."

He opened the false bed of the chuckwagon and took out two rifles. One was a Henry, the other a Winchester Yellow Boy. Both were chambered for the .44 Henry round.

Kelly loaded his, and Liza did the same. He looked at her and said, "If this comes down to shooting, you find yourself some good cover, all right?"

"Yes, sir."

Suddenly Kelly felt old. His back began to ache, and a sense of exhaustion washed over him. "All right," he said with a sigh. "You ride around the far side of the herd and get the men to start coming in for their rifles. I'll do this side."

"Yes, sir, Pa."

* * *

The wrangler had saddled two horses for them earlier, so all they had to do was mount up and go. The first rider Kelly came across was Pullen, his ramrod. It was the first time he'd seen him that morning.

"How did you go with that cow?"

"All fine, Mr. Kelly."

"Good. But you haven't eaten this morning."

Pullen shook his head. "No, sir. When I came back, I took over riding nighthawk."

"Go and get something from the Reverend," Kelly ordered. "And pick up a rifle."

"You expecting trouble?"

Kelly shook his head. "No sense in not being prepared if it comes along."

Kelly stayed out with the herd until one of his men fetched him half an hour later. "Mr. Kelly, you're wanted at the river crossing."

Kelly rode to the river, Pullen and Liza riding with him. He stopped at the water's edge and there they were, the twenty men from the previous day.

"What did you decide, Kelly?" Miles called to the trail boss.

"Yes, what did we decide, Pa?" Liza asked her father.

"All right, you can look over the herd. But only you and two other men."

"You seem to think you have some kind of bargaining power in this, Kelly," Miles called.

"Those are my terms," the trail boss replied. "All of my men are armed with rifles. If we need to, I'll stampede my herd across this river, and we'll see how many men you're willing to lose."

Miles was quiet for a period of time before he said, "All right. I'll agree to that."

The man kneed his horse forward. He was followed by two others. The animals splashed through the water, their passage creating white foam that was whipped downstream on the current. As their horses climbed the other bank, they drew them to a halt. Miles said, pointing to the cattle inspector, "This is Crown. He's the inspector. This other gent is my man, Rio Wade."

Kelly nodded in the direction of the herd. "The cattle are that way."

The six riders rode to where the cowboys held the herd. Kelly, Pullen, and Liza stopped and let the three newcomers ride around the animals.

As they did so, Miles said quietly, "I don't see that steer you brought here, Rio."

The gunman looked around, his head moving left and right. "It should be. When we released it, the damn thing was headed straight for them."

"Do you see it, Crown?"

There was a hint of relief in the man's voice when he replied, "No, I don't."

"Keep looking. It has to be here somewhere."

For the next thirty minutes, the riders wove through the herd, looking for the sick steer that was meant to be there, but came up empty-handed.

"You men done?" Kelly asked as they came by once more.

The three men drew in, and Miles stared at him. He looked angry. "I guess your herd is fine."

"Does that mean we can cross, Mister Inspector?"

The small man nodded vigorously. "Yes, yes, indeed."

Kelly turned to Pullen. "Get them moving, Ben."

The trail boss turned back to look at Miles, who still had a smoldering expression on his face. Kelly said, "If you gents don't mind, we've got work to do."

* * *

By the time Miles returned to the other side of the river, he was livid. He turned his anger on Wade. "What happened? Where was that damned cow?"

The gunman shrugged. "They must have found it and got rid of it."

Miles turned and looked at the cattle inspector. "Go away."

The man looked perplexed. "What?"

"I don't need you anymore. Go."

As the inspector rode off, Miles said to his troubleshooter, "I did not ride all the way down here to have this happen. Understood?"

"What do you want me to do?"

"Stampede their herd. Make sure none of them survive. Those cows don't go to Abilene."

"Yes, sir."

Miles saw the question on his face. "The girl too, Rio. No one lives to tell the tale."

"Got it."

* * *

That night the chill breeze swept across the plain, and Liza pulled her coat up higher around the back of her neck. The rocking motion of the horse beneath her created a hypnotic effect that threatened to put her to sleep after the long day in the saddle, but it was her turn to ride nighthawk, and she wouldn't be treated differently than any of the hands.

Liza started to sing, a low melodic tone that seemed to ease the uncertainty of the cattle. To the west, there was a flash of lightning and the distant rumble of thunder. A few of the cattle moved restlessly and started to mill. This wasn't good.

Pullen appeared out of the darkness and eased his

horse in beside hers. "That storm is getting closer."

"Yes, and the cattle are getting skittish," Liza replied. "I think there is a good chance they'll run."

"I'll get everyone up," Pullen told her and swung his horse away from hers.

A sudden peal of thunder split the night, except it wasn't thunder but the whiplash of a rifle. The ramrod toppled sideways from his saddle. Liza's head snapped around to look in the direction of the shot. The rifle fired again, and this time she saw the muzzle flash, like a crimson flower blooming in the darkness.

The bullet fanned her face, causing her to hunch low over the saddle. She kicked her horse hard, and the cow pony responded by lunging into a run.

More shots cracked out, and the rounds passed above Liza as she kicked her pony again. Off to her left, the cattle were starting to bellow loudly. Then they began to move as one like a wave across the ground.

In front of her, Liza saw a rider loom out of the darkness. For a moment she thought it was one of the other hands, but it wasn't. The rider fired at her with his rifle, and the bullet cracked as it passed close overhead. She sawed on the reins, and the horse beneath her turned to the right and started to run away from the stampeding herd.

Liza galloped through the darkness and hadn't gone much farther before disaster struck. The pony beneath her stumbled, fought to right itself, and then went down hard. Liza was tossed over its neck.

The young woman hit the ground hard, and lights

flashed before her eyes. The air whooshed from her lungs, and she cartwheeled across the hard earth. She skidded to a stop, her arms and legs splayed. Liza rolled over and tried to rise, unwilling to remain there for any length of time in case the careening herd turned in her direction.

She managed to gain her feet before the world began spinning wildly. In front of her, a rider appeared on a snorting horse. She looked up at him, her vision blurred—not that it mattered in the dark. The rider raised a six-gun in his fist and pointed it at Liza's head. Before the rider could fire a shot, Liza took a couple of lurching steps to the right before falling to the ground, and she didn't move again.

* * *

It was daylight when consciousness seeped back into Liza's head. The sun was high overhead, and when she opened her eyes, the brightness made the dull ache inside her head explode.

Rolling onto her side, Liza moaned and cracked an eyelid but saw nothing except blades of dry grass. She raised her head slightly, then sat up. With her hands pressed to her head, she tried to remember what had happened. The grass was wet; she was wet. Rain?

Then everything flooded back.

"Pa," she gasped and clawed her way to her feet. The world spun, but Liza remained on her feet through grim determination. She saw her horse lying on its side, unmoving. She felt a pang in her heart when she saw it; it had been a good animal, and she'd ridden it many times since leaving Texas.

Liza gathered her bearings and started in the direction of the camp, her boots sinking in the soft, wet earth. The range was dotted with the lumps of dead cattle. When she reached the chuckwagon, she found one man waiting sullenly—the cowboy called Hawk.

"Where's Pa? Where's everyone else?" she asked.

Hawk shook his head and said, "We're it, Miss Liza. There's nobody else left."

A wave of dread washed over her. "Pa?"

"He's gone. I saw his horse fall in front of the herd. Have you seen Ben? He's the only one I couldn't find."

Liza dropped her face into her hands as the news about her father sank in.

"Miss Liza, Ben?"

Liza looked up, her cheeks streaked with tears. She frowned. "Ben?"

"Yes, miss. Have you seen him?"

Instead of answering his question, she said, "The riders. Did you see the riders?"

"What riders?"

"The ones with the herd. One of them shot Ben and tried to shoot me."

"You sure, Miss Liza? I never saw any riders. Just the cattle."

"There were riders, I tell you. They stampeded the cattle."

"That was the storm," Hawk told her.

"No. You must have seen them."

"No, miss."

"You must have."

"No."

Suddenly dizzy again, Liza staggered, and Hawk hurried to keep her steady. He caught her in his arms as her legs buckled and she fainted.

* * *

It wasn't until the following day that Liza woke again. The pain in her skull was still there but had dulled slightly. Hawk offered her his canteen of water, which she sipped and then laid back.

"Where are we?" she asked.

"Still where we were yesterday," the man replied.

"What about the cattle?"

"They're not there."

"What?"

"They've gone. The rain from the storm washed out all sign."

"Surely they couldn't have gone far. The best part of two thousand head can't just vanish."

Hawk nodded. "I thought the same as you, Miss Liza, but it looks like you were right."

"About what?"

"For them to disappear like that, there had to have been riders who took them."

"So, we've lost the herd?"

"It looks that way, yes."

"Then we need to find them."

"How?" Hawk asked. "They could be anywhere, and we're only two."

"We have to try."

"If we catch up, what then?"

"I don't know," Liza admitted.

Hawk thought for a moment. "We could go to Abilene and hire some men to come back and look."

"Hire men? What with?"

"There was some money in the chuckwagon, and there are the rifles. We could sell them for more."

"By the time we did that, the cattle would be long gone."

"Then what?" Hawk asked. "What do we do?"

"We go to Abilene and hope we can learn something there. But first, we need to get the shovel from the chuckwagon so we can bury our dead."

Chapter 3

"What do you mean, you're leaving?" Joseph McCoy asked the three cattle buyers standing in front of him.

"We were here to buy a herd, and it's not coming," the rotund Carter Lewis replied.

"Miss Kelly can't help it if it was stolen," McCoy reminded them. "Besides, there'll be others."

"Can you guarantee they won't be diseased, Joe?"

"Oh, not that again," McCoy growled, running a hand through his dark hair. He had thin, intense features and a goatee jutting from his chin. "I'm telling you, there is no Texas Fever in the herds that are coming north."

"That's not what we're hearing," Frank Beaumont said.

"Those are just stories started by Hank Miles from over at Ellsworth. Nothing else. Come over to the Drover's Cottage. I'll buy you all a drink, and we can talk about it some more."

"It's a waste of time, Joe," Lewis said. "The train

comes through in an hour, and we're going to be on it."

"Damn it, what about the other herds?"

"You'll just have to find other buyers for them."

McCoy's jaw set firm. "You know what? That's just what I'll do. You three can go to hell."

McCoy stormed off toward the three-story Drover's Cottage. The hotel was an extravagance. It had plastered walls and green Venetian blinds, plus other fancy fixings. It was also home to a saloon and billiard parlor. The rooms could sleep eighty guests, and the dining room could seat and cater to more than two hundred. Then there was the large barn that had been constructed to house up to a hundred horses.

Abilene was still growing, the evidence all around in the new frame buildings that were under construction.

McCoy went to the bar and grabbed a bottle before walking to a table he frequented more often lately. He poured a drink and threw it down in one swallow, then slammed the glass on the tabletop out of pure frustration.

"Damn it."

"Trouble, sugar?" asked a melodic voice with more than a hint of a Southern accent.

McCoy looked up into the painted face of a curvaceous, dark-haired woman. He poured himself another drink.

"Grab yourself a glass, Sally, and I'll tell you all about it."

"That's the best offer I've had all day, sugar."

She walked over to the bar, hips swaying

seductively as she went. McCoy watched her go, staring at the back of her dress. When she returned, she placed a glass beside the bottle and said, "Pour me a drink, baby."

The bottle chinked on the glass as he slopped the pale brown liquid into it. Once it was full, Sally picked it up and studied the contents with her round brown eyes before tossing it back.

She placed the empty glass on the table and looked at McCoy. He gestured at the bottle. "Help yourself."

Sally leaned forward, her large, pale breasts threatening to spill out of the bodice of her emerald green dress. "Where are the other girls?" McCoy asked.

"Still in bed," Sally replied. "If I can't get any attention, they sure as hell can't. You ain't looking for any company, are you, Joe?"

"How about I pay you a visit tonight? After today, I might be needing something to cheer me up."

"Why?"

"The cattle buyers are leaving."

Sally drank her second drink and slumped back in the chair. "I thought *I* was having a tough day. Honey, you'll be needing some company tonight."

"What I need is something to garner attention. Something that's sure to bring in the buyers."

"Pity you can't ship some buffalo to the markets instead of Longhorns," Sally said. "There's plenty of them west of here."

The suggestion, not intended to be serious, began to germinate in McCoy's brain. His thoughts took a while to come together, but when they did, McCoy's face split in a big grin.

"Sally, you're a wonder," he exclaimed as he slapped a hand down on the table.

"What did I do?" she asked, startled by his reaction.

"You, my dear, just gave me the best idea ever."

"I did?"

He got up from his chair and kissed her hard on the lips, then drew back and said, "I'll see you tonight, darling."

* * *

McCoy grabbed his hat and hurried to the telegraph office. Pushing through the door, he moved to the counter and began writing his message on a slip of paper with the stub of pencil provided. His wire was sent to the head office at the Hannibal and St. Joseph Railroad, requesting a locomotive and two stock cars. He also asked that extra timber be shipped with it.

He waited until a return message came in, asking why he needed it. McCoy replied, *Have an idea to get buyers back. If it works, Abilene will boom. Need what I asked for. If not, Abilene will die.*

Ten minutes later, another wire came through. *Will send as requested. Expect within week.*

Happy with the reply, McCoy began making plans as he left the telegraph office.

Soon after McCoy left, the telegrapher sent another message. *McCoy up to something. Just sent word to head office requesting a locomotive and two stock cars. Will keep you posted.*

* * *

Creed had received orders to meet Faraday in St. Louis. The Texan hated the big city—the crowds, the way people stared at him as though he were some sort of savage because he dressed in range clothes and wore a holstered revolver openly. It was evident when he walked into the lavish four-story Planter's House Hotel on Fourth and Pine.

Creed warily approached the counter in the lobby, looking around before leaning his rifle against the dark-timber-paneled front. Standing behind the highly polished top were two young men, one with his hair slicked to one side in an unnatural way. Creed smiled at the pair. "Howdy, gents."

One of the two young men stepped forward, his face as pinched as though his mother had made him suck lemons every day as a boy. "I believe, sir, that you may well be in the wrong establishment."

The Texan stared at him for a moment before saying, "This is the Planter's House, isn't it?"

"It is, sir."

"Then I'm in the right place."

Creed's flat tone left little room for argument, but he got one anyway. The second desk clerk stepped forward and said, "I don't think you understand, sir. This hotel does not cater to...to..."

Creed finished the sentence for him. "People like me?"

"I'm sorry, sir, but since you put it that way, yes. The hotel accommodates people of standing. We've had President Lincoln stay here, as well as Andrew

Jackson. We serve boiled grouse, fried oysters, and custard and apples. Our rooms run almost five dollars per night. Do you understand now, sir?"

The Texan nodded. "I believe I do. I'll take that room now."

"I'm sorry, sir, but—"

The clerk stopped when Creed picked up his Yellow Boy and laid it flat on the counter. "Now. Please."

"Is there a problem here?" a voice asked from behind Creed.

The Texan turned to see Matthew Faraday standing a few feet away. One of the young clerks cleared his throat and said, "No problem, Mr. Faraday. We were just explaining to the gentleman that he might be more suited elsewhere."

"I see," Faraday said, running his steely gaze over Creed. "He does look like a ruffian, doesn't he? He looks like he's been dragged through a mesquite patch by a cow pony. Would that be a fair assessment, gentlemen?"

"More than fair, in my opinion," one of the clerks agreed with a sniff.

Creed placed his hand on the rifle and said, "I'd be careful about what comes out of your mouth next. Might be that your teeth will come with it."

The clerk's mouth dropped open, and he shot Faraday an alarmed look. The older man grinned and patted Creed on the shoulder.

"I think you can let the man keep his teeth, John. It's good to see you."

Creed kept his gaze on the clerk as he said, "It's

good to see you, too, sir."

The second clerk swallowed hard and said, "This is your man, Mr. Faraday?"

Faraday nodded. "He is. I asked him to come here. We have business to discuss, so if you don't mind, I'm sure you can find him a room. Preferably somewhere on my floor?"

"Yes, sir. Right away."

Faraday smiled. "Thank you. Join me for supper tonight, John."

"Yes, sir."

Faraday was about to leave when he caught Creed looking across the foyer at a man dressed in a suit and top hat who was standing talking to another man who was similarly attired. Beside him was a younger lady—his daughter from the looks of her. She wore a pale pink dress and her gaze was openly directed at the Texan.

"Stay away from her, John," Faraday cautioned. "She's the daughter of the richest man in St. Louis. If you go anywhere near her, he'll have his men hunting the streets high and low for you with orders to skin you alive."

"Just admiring the view, sir."

"Are you sure that's all *she* is doing?"

"I couldn't tell you what goes on in a woman's mind, sir."

Faraday grunted. "Don't be late for dinner."

"Yes, sir."

"And wear something appropriate," Faraday said.

Creed stared at his boss and said, "You hired me for what I can do, not what I wear. If you don't like it, I'll just find a saloon somewhere and eat there."

Faraday's eyes flashed. "You still have a sharp tongue, I see. Maybe too sharp for your own good."

"I'm glad to see nothing has changed since the last time we spoke, Mr. Faraday." Creed picked up the key one of the clerks slid across the counter to him, engraved with the number 17. "I'll see you at suppertime."

With that, Creed took his rifle and walked toward the stairs.

He didn't know where Room 17 was, but he was a pretty good tracker. He figured he could find it.

* * *

The dining room was huge. In all his travels, Creed had never seen anything as big or extravagant. He took in the three large chandeliers that hung from the ornately plastered ceiling and the dark wood wainscoting that adorned the lower half of every wall. Art of all kinds had been hung over the patterned wallpaper, and brass lamp fixtures were evenly spaced around the room to provide even more light.

The tables spread throughout the room were topped with stark white tablecloths and shiny silver cutlery. As Creed looked around, he muttered, "Well, I'll be a son of a—"

"Can I help you, sir?"

Creed turned to face a man dressed in a black suit with an immaculate white shirt beneath. The Texan looked at him and asked, "Who are you?"

"The maître d', sir."

"The what?"

"The individual who will show you to your seat. However..."

"What?" Creed asked.

"You might be able to scrape by in what you are wearing, sir, but you will need a tie."

Creed rolled his eyes. "You're joshing me, right?"

"Oh, dear." The man sighed. "I can assure you, sir, I am not *joshing* you. And the gun will have to go."

Creed's eyes narrowed. "If you want it, take it."

The maître d' sighed again. "Come with me, sir."

The Texan shrugged. "You're the boss."

They walked across to a small, chest-high desk, and the man went behind it and bent to rifle through a drawer. When he stood up, he held out a tie in his hand. "Take this, sir. Put it on, and you should be fine."

Creed took it. "You want me to bring it back here when I'm done?"

The maître d' wrinkled his nose and said, "Keep it, sir. It may come in handy one day should you wish to hang yourself with it."

A broad smile split Creed's face. "I like you. What's your name?"

"Benson, sir."

"Well, Benson, after I finish my meal, how about we get a drink?"

"I'd rather roll in a cholla patch, sir."

"Ha!" Creed chuckled. "I'm here to dine with Mr. Faraday."

"I'll show you to your table."

Benson led the way to the far side of the room between many rows of tables before stopping at the one where Faraday was seated across from a mustachioed gentleman and a woman in a blue dress. Faraday looked up at the new arrivals and said, "Thank you, Benson. I hope he didn't give you too much trouble?"

"Nothing I couldn't handle, sir."

The man left for his station, and Faraday said, "I see he couldn't pry that horse pistol away from you."

"Not for want of trying, sir," Creed growled as he tried to fix the tie. "Blasted thing."

"Here, let me help," the woman said, getting out of her seat.

"I can do it, ma'am," Creed said hurriedly.

She batted his hands away. "Nonsense. You'll be there all day."

"Don't argue with her, son. When she gets like this, Gloria means business."

Creed looked into the woman's striking blue eyes, then took in the rest of her flawless face. Apparently, she was a lot younger than he had figured at first.

"There, all done," she said with a broad smile that revealed two rows of even white teeth. In a softer voice, she said, "Let me know if there is anything else I can do for you."

Creed swallowed hard. "Yes, ma'am."

Once he took his seat at the table, Faraday began to speak, "Now that is out of the way, I'll introduce our guests. This is Kenneth and Gloria Travers. Ken is the president of the Hannibal and St. Joseph Railroad. This is John Creed. He may look a little rough around the edges, but be assured, he's one of my best agents."

"I must say, son," Travers said, "your boss is right. You don't look like much."

"I could say the same about you, sir," Creed shot back.

Gloria Travers smirked at that retort while Faraday pressed his lips together.

After a moment, Travers nodded. "You might do. I like a man who isn't afraid to say what he thinks."

"As long as we understand each other."

"I believe we do."

"Now that is over with," Faraday said, "shall we order?"

Creed picked up a menu and began to study the list of dishes.

"You can read, Mr. Creed?"

Even though she might not have meant it that way, Gloria Travers' tone was condescending. Although the tone and the question irked the Texan, he didn't let it bother him. He responded with a grin, "I can do a lot of things, ma'am."

Let her make of that whatever she wanted to, Creed thought.

"I must apologize," she said. "That sounded appalling and was not what I intended."

"No offense taken, ma'am."

"Ken, I think I would like fried oysters this evening."

"As you wish, my dear."

Settling her gaze on Creed, her look became bolder. The Texan shifted uncomfortably in his chair and hastily returned his eyes to the menu. After ordering, they drank and chatted amiably about numerous topics until their meals arrived.

Once they were finished and the plates cleared away, Faraday said, "Let's get down to business. John, Ken has come to me for help. I'll let him fill you in on the problem."

Travers nodded. "Thank you, Matt. Creed, our company has a contract with Joseph McCoy of Abilene to ship all the cattle he can supply us with back east. The Kansas Pacific put in a switch for him, as well as a siding. McCoy built the yards, and we have invested quite a substantial amount of money in helping him out. However, with the growing talk of Texas Fever, things have changed. Then, just over a week back, a whole herd was stampeded and vanished."

"What has that got to do with the agency?"

"I'm getting to that," Travers said. "A few days later, the buyers left Abilene, even though they were assured that more herds would be coming north. The fear of Texas Fever is killing the town, and it is all driven by a man named Hank Miles."

"What does he have to do with it?"

"Miles holds a monopoly over all the herds that trail to Ellsworth. If Abilene proved to be fruitful, then I guess he stands to lose a lot of money."

"I still don't understand what this has to do with me."

"McCoy came to us with an idea to bring the buyers back to Abilene, only it's going to cost us more money and equipment."

"What did you say?" Creed asked.

"What could we say? We said yes. It was either that, or we would lose more money than we can afford to. That was the reason I approached Matthew. We need someone to watch over whatever it is McCoy has planned. Matt recommended you."

"What is it exactly that McCoy has planned?" Creed asked, his interest piqued.

"We're not sure," Travers replied. "We just know what he requested from us. Not that it matters. Whatever it is, it has to succeed."

The Texan looked at Faraday.

"Well?" the agency owner asked.

"I'll do it," Creed said. The situation was just curious enough to interest him. "Does he know I'm coming?"

"No," Travers said with a shake of his head. "We'll leave it up to you whether you tell him or not. Matthew thought you might prefer to keep your business in Abilene a secret, at least starting out."

"Fair enough. When do I leave?"

"Tomorrow," Faraday told him. "There's a train in the morning. The locomotive and the stock cars McCoy has requested will leave the day after."

"I want the train to drop me a couple of miles outside of Abilene. I'll ride in like everybody else."

The agency owner said, "I can organize that."

"I guess we're good then," Creed said. "At least until I find out what McCoy has in mind."

* * *

The knock on Creed's door was light yet firm. He frowned at it before swinging his legs off the bed and placing his feet on the floor. He stood up and padded across the large rug to the door.

"Who is it?"

"I came to see if you needed help with your tie... or anything else," the voice from the other side said.

Gloria Travers. This was not good. No, this was bad. He opened the door. She stood there, wearing the same dress she'd worn at dinner. "Are you going to ask me in?"

Creed hesitantly stepped aside so she could cross the threshold. "Shouldn't you be with your husband?"

"He's with your boss. They'll be talking business and drinking at the gentlemen's club for hours. I told him I was going to bed."

Closing the door, Creed asked bluntly, "Did you tell him who with?"

"Oh, that must have slipped my mind."

Gloria stepped closer to Creed and stopped in front of him, close enough that her ample breasts were almost touching his chest. She turned her face up to his and gave him a seductive look as she asked, "Would you like to help me out of my dress?"

Creed raised his eyebrows. "As much as that would please me, I'm working for your husband. I have a rule about mixing business and pleasure."

She pouted at him. "Are you sure? I could—"

"I'm sure," he said, cutting her off. "I'm sorry, Mrs. Travers, but as much as I want to, I can't."

Gathering what was left of her dignity, she said, "Perhaps another time then. When you aren't working for Kenneth."

"Maybe."

Creed opened the door and let her out before closing and locking it behind her. For a moment, he couldn't help but think he'd just dodged a bullet.

* * *

The following morning, he met up with Faraday for breakfast, and they ate a hearty meal of bacon, eggs, and biscuits. Once they were finished, Faraday sat back before reaching into his suit pocket to retrieve a small money roll. He handed it to Creed. "There's two hundred dollars in there. It should be sufficient for your needs."

"Thank you, sir."

"I heard about Lucky Theron. That was a good job. Except for the part where you weren't supposed to go into the town on your own."

"It worked out all right."

"This time, John," the agency owner said. "What about next time?"

"I'll worry about that when the time comes."

"Listen, I did my own digging about Miles," Faraday told him. "He's one to be wary of. Has a bunch of hard cases and gun-wolves working for him. One of them is named Rio Wade. He's wanted in a couple of places, but for some reason, he's still walking around. Be careful around him and any others on Miles' payroll."

"Yes, sir. What about the law?"

"There is none."

"All right."

"If you need anything, help is only a telegraph message away."

"I'll be fine, sir."

"Good. One last thing." Faraday gave him a solemn look. "You did right last night, turning away Mrs. Travers. It would have become needlessly complicated."

Creed opened his mouth to speak, but Faraday held up a hand. "I know everything. It's my job."

* * *

"I want to know what McCoy is up to," Miles growled. "Take a few of the boys over there and find out what you can. Make things difficult."

Rio Wade nodded. "How difficult?"

"As difficult as need be."

"What about the cattle we rustled?" Wade asked.

"They'll be shipped to Chicago in a few days. Once the brands have been altered, I'll have them brought to the yards, ready for shipping."

"You're not worried about what happens at the other end? What if they ask questions?"

Miles shrugged. "Does it matter? I have a bill of sale."

"Sure," Wade said. "I'll let the boys know."

"I have a lot of money riding on this, Rio. Don't let me down."

Chapter 4

Creed entered Abilene late in the afternoon. He rode in from the east along the rail line. The train that had dropped him outside of town was long gone by the time he arrived, so he appeared to be just another drifter on horseback.

The Texan found the livery stable on the north side of the tracks, not far from the Great Western Stockyards office. He dismounted outside and was met by a dark-haired man with a more than welcoming demeanor.

"Help you, stranger?"

"Sure. Need a stall for my horse for a few days, maybe a week."

The man nodded. "Ed Gaylord can do anything."

"That's you, huh?"

"Sure is. This is my place."

Creed looked at it again. "It's big."

"Yes, sir. Double the size of a normal livery. Needs to be, with all the cowboys coming this way."

"I heard there was some trouble with one of

the herds?"

Gaylord nodded. "That's right. Rustlers. Took the Kelly herd. Killed all but two of the hands who were with it. Kelly hisself got plowed under in the stampede."

Creed winced. They hadn't told him the part about most of the crew being killed. "Any idea who was responsible?"

"Nope. Not really." Gaylord looked at him curiously. "Say, are you from Texas?"

Creed nodded. "Yeah."

The hostler smiled, exposing yellowed teeth. "I knowed you was. Can tell you Texans from a mile away."

"Are there more herds coming up the Chisholm?"

"Sure, there are. But it won't do them no good if they get here."

"Why is that?"

"No buyers."

Gaylord took the horse and led it inside. The stable smelled of horses and fresh hay. He didn't need to go far to find an empty stall. He took the Yellow Boy from the scabbard and passed it to Creed before putting the horse in the vacant stall. Then he undid the cinch, removed the saddle from the buckskin, and said, "I can store your saddle for an extra five cents a day."

The Texan shrugged. "Sure, why not?" Creed paid the man and asked, "Where's a good place to stay?"

"You could try the Drover's Cottage or the Longhorn. It's over on Cedar Street."

"I might try there."

"If I was you, I'd try the Cottage. The Longhorn is a mite pricey if you know what I mean."

"I guess I do. You know of any work around these parts?"

"You might check with McCoy. He'll be over at the Cottage."

"I'll do that."

As Creed grabbed his saddlebags and prepared to leave the livery, four men rode through the doors. Gaylord took one look at them and was immediately on edge. They stared openly at Creed as they entered, trying, the Texan guessed, to intimidate him in some way. They drew up and dismounted.

"Howdy, Gaylord," said a solid man with a scar on his cheek. "I need to put up these broncs for a day or two."

"You going to pay me this time, Wade?" the liveryman asked.

The man gave him a wicked smile and said, "We'll see."

At the mention of the man's name, Creed turned to stare. Wade must have sensed it because he looked at the Texan and asked, "Something wrong, stranger?"

Creed shrugged. "I guess not."

"Then what are you looking at?" another man growled.

Creed ignored him and turned around to walk out.

"I'm talking to you, mister."

"I'm not talking to you," Creed called over his shoulder and disappeared outside into the afternoon sun.

He crossed the tracks and walked past the Drover's Cottage. From there, he sauntered along Cedar Street until he found the Longhorn. Creed went inside and was astounded by what he found. The hardwood bar was against the north wall, a brass footrail along its base. There was a large mirror behind the back bar, and paintings of bawdy women graced most of the walls. Everywhere you looked was an abundance of gaming tables. The problem being, there were no cowboys to play them.

Creed walked up to the bar and was greeted by a tall, thin man wearing a white shirt. "Something I can do for you, stranger?"

"I'd like a room."

"Cost you two dollars a night."

Creed looked at him without blinking. "I only want a room, not the whole damn saloon."

"Take it or leave it, friend." The Texan turned to leave, and the bartender hastily said, "Hold on. I guess we can do some kind of deal."

"Fifty cents," Creed said.

The saloonkeeper's eyes bulged. "Now, wait just a damn minute—"

"Looks to me like rooms aren't exactly in high demand right now."

The man sighed. "All right." He grabbed a key from under the counter and tossed it to Creed. "Room eight. Money up front."

The Texan dug into his pocket and took out a dollar. "Here, this'll be a start."

* * *

It was dark when Creed emerged from the Longhorn. He was hungry, and instead of tempting fate and eating in the saloon, he decided to settle for some home cooking if he could find a good café.

Ten minutes later, he was seated in a small eatery with several tables scattered throughout a long room. Although it seemed unusual that a café in a town the size of Abilene was as quiet as this, he wasn't the only one there. At another table sat a young woman and a man, both wearing range clothes, which got Creed's attention. It wasn't often you came across a woman dressed like a cowboy and armed with a Colt.

He ordered steak and potatoes with gravy. While he waited for the meal, he drank black coffee. The food was delicious, and there was plenty of it. When the dark-haired waitress came to take his plate after he was finished, she asked, "Would you like some dessert, mister?"

"What do you have?"

"Deep-dish apple pie."

Creed smiled. "Sounds good. I'll have another cup of coffee while I wait."

"Coming right up."

She left, and while Creed waited for her to return with the coffee pot, the door to the café opened, and in walked three of the four men he'd seen over at the livery. All three were raucous until they spotted the two seated at the table.

He watched as the one he'd had words with walked over to the man and woman and stood near their table. Creed heard him ask, "How's that herd of yours?"

"Go away," the young woman said.

"Heard tell you had some trouble." He cackled as he looked at his friends.

"I said, go away."

"You heard the lady," the man seated with her said.

But the troublemaker wasn't done yet. Behind him, his friends spread out, and Creed immediately thought, "ambush." The troublemaker said, his voice full of menace, "I weren't talking to you, Tex. I'm talking to Miss Kelly here."

So that was it, Creed thought. She was the daughter of the trail boss who'd lost his herd and his life. What did these men have to do with it?

The man with her stood up and grabbed his hat before saying, "Come on, Liza, let's go."

The troublemaker moved to cut them off. "Sit down, Tex. We was just being friendly. No need to rush—"

He turned and saw Creed looking on. "Well, well, well. Look who we have here."

The Texan eased his hand down toward his Colt. The troublemaker started walking in his direction.

"We meet again."

Creed just stared at him.

"Still not talking to me? That's just downright rude."

The waitress appeared once more, bringing out the coffee. Seeing the possible confrontation, she left it on the table and backed away quickly. The troublemaker stared at the coffee pot and said, "You know what? I might just sit here with you and have me a cup of that there coffee."

"How about you find your own table?" Creed suggested in a low voice.

The troublemaker smiled and turned to his friends. "He does talk."

He reached out to grab the chair when Creed's low voice stopped him. "I'll give you one chance, mister, because I think you're hard of hearing. But if you grab the back of that chair, you might just lose a finger."

The man's smile grew cold. "You almost got me scared, mister."

Creed said nothing, although he was aware of every eye in the room on him. The troublemaker glanced at his friends again. One said, "Go on, Slim. Pour me a cup, too."

"Why not?"

As soon as his hand touched the back of the seat, the Colt came clear of Creed's holster. The barrel poked above the table, and the weapon crashed. Wood from the back of the chair splintered, and the man's hand flew away. Looking down at his paw, he saw that where he used to have five fingers, there were now only four.

The troublemaker's eyes grew wide as blood began to flow from the ruined hand. "Ah! You shot my damn finger off!"

Creed came to his feet, a thin line of bluish smoke rising from the barrel of the Colt. "You were warned, mister," the Texan said. "Maybe next time you want to impress your friends, you might think twice about doing it."

Slim's face twisted into a mask of rage. "I'm going

to kill you for that, you son of a bitch."

"You might want to get yourself another trigger finger before you try."

Holding his hand, trying to stem the flow of blood, Slim snarled, "This ain't over."

"My back will be expecting you."

The cowboys walked toward the door, Slim leaving a trail of blood a blind man could follow.

"Hey," Creed called as he reached down to the floor and scooped something up. "You forgot this."

They looked at him, and he held up his hand.

He wiggled Slim's trigger finger a couple of times, then tossed it on the table.

Slim growled another curse and snapped at one of his friends, "Go get it."

The man shook his head. "I'm not touchin' that. Get it yourself."

"I would, but I'm busy trying not to bleed to death here!"

"That ain't going to kill you."

"Just get the damned thing, will you?"

The man grimaced, then went to the table and picked up the finger as though it were some kind of diseased lump of meat he might catch something from. He walked over to Slim and tucked it into his pocket. The wounded cowboy glared at him, then they opened the door to the café and left.

The waitress appeared, and he said to her, "I'm sorry about the mess, miss."

"Do you, uh, still want your dessert?"

He smiled at her. "Thank you, that would be fine. I was looking forward to it."

While she was gone, the man and woman at the other table went back to talking for a moment before they both stood up and walked toward him.

"Mind if we join you?" the young woman asked.

"Sure. You might want to find another chair, though."

The man moved the blood-splattered one aside and grabbed a second ladderback chair for the woman. When they were both seated, they looked across the table at him.

"To what do I owe the pleasure?" Creed asked.

"I'm Liza Kelly," the woman said. She indicated the dark-haired man on her right. "This is Jack Hawk. We were wondering if you came up the trail?"

"No, ma'am."

"Oh."

"Are you the people who lost the herd?" Creed asked.

"We didn't catch your name, mister," Hawk said.

"John Creed."

"It seems we three have something in common," Liza said.

"How's that?"

"We all know those troublemakers who work for Hank Miles."

Creed shook his head. "I only ran into them in the livery. Up until then, I had no idea they were even alive."

"You're from Texas," Liza observed.

"Yes, ma'am."

"Whereabouts?"

"Little place outside of Waco. What happened

64

to your herd?"

Liza told him.

"You figure this Miles put the sick cow in your herd?"

Hawk said, "The more we think about it, the more it makes sense. Since we've been in Abilene, all we hear are stories about Miles and how much he hates the town."

"What are you still doing in Abilene?" Creed asked.

"Trying to find out what happened to our herd," Liza told him.

"If you ask me, you're going about it all wrong."

"Really?" Hawk commented. "How would you do it?"

"Go straight to the source of the problem," the Texan told them. "Ellsworth would be the place I'd start. From what you've said, the man has the means and ability to pull it off."

Hawk and Liza glanced at each other. "We never thought of it like that," she said.

"The other thing is, if he's had your cattle that long, then there's a good chance they've already been shipped east. Have there been any trains through lately?"

"No. We were the first of the herds up the trail this season. There's two more coming in over the next couple of days. There will be more behind them, but with no buyers and the rumor of Texas Fever—"

Creed nodded. "It'll kill the town if McCoy has no cattle buyers. Before it even gets started."

"That's right."

"I heard McCoy has a plan to get the buyers back."

Hawk grunted and shook his head. "If you can call it a plan."

"That bad?" Creed asked.

Liza said, "He plans on heading west to the buffalo grounds, rounding some up, and shipping them back east to Chicago."

Creed stared at her for a moment, running the idea through his head. "What? Why would he do that?"

"I have no idea."

"I guess he'll be needing help to get it done," the Texan mused.

"Surely you aren't thinking of asking to hire on for such a foolhardy idea?" Liza asked.

He smiled at her and saw her eyes light up when he did so. "Sure, I am. Cowboy has to eat. And I need the work."

"Well, Mr. Creed, I wish you luck."

* * *

"You idiots just couldn't stay out of trouble, could you?" Wade growled as he shuffled the large-bladed knife around in the fire he'd made. After a minute, he pulled it out of the coals and looked at the glowing tip.

"What you going to do with that?" Slim asked.

"What the hell you think I'm going to do with it?" Wade growled.

"No, you ain't going to do—"

His words were cut off as his friends grabbed hold of him.

"Hell, Rio, don't do it," the outlaw pleaded.

"Have to, Slim. It'll get infected otherwise. Hold him still."

Wade took the hand in a vice-like grip, and Slim whimpered as the blade got closer to the stump of the missing finger. The blade seared what was left, cauterizing the blood vessels and eliciting a howl of pain.

The smell of scorched flesh rose, permeating the air, and caused Wade to wrinkle his nose at the offensive stench.

"You can let him go now," he growled. "Get a rag on it to keep out the dirt. You'll have to learn to shoot left-handed."

Slim looked up, his eyes filled with pain and anger. "I'll learn to shoot. Don't you worry about that. And when I do, I'm going to kill that bastard."

Chapter 5

Creed walked into the Drover's Cottage saloon and looked around. Perhaps ten people were inside. Once the herds arrived, that number would shoot up, but if the buyers failed to return, the rest of the trail-drive season would be a bust.

A couple of customers looked up from their tables and gave him a cursory and disinterested glance before returning to their conversations. The first person to pay him real attention was a lushly-built dark-haired woman in a low-cut dress. Judging by her looks and clothes, paying attention to the customers was her job. She strutted across to where Creed stood, her chest thrust out to gain his attention.

"You look like you could use a drink, cowboy."

"I could use work more," he said.

"Oh?"

"Is McCoy around?"

The whore's shoulders slumped. "How the hell am I supposed to make any money around this joint?"

Creed looked at her questioningly.

She waved a hand at him. "Never mind. It's been a long evening. Follow me."

She showed him over to a table, where McCoy was seated with a half-empty bottle. He looked up at them both with bleary eyes and asked, "What do you want?"

Creed glanced at the woman. "He always like this?"

"Only since he saw his dream going up in flames."

"I thought he had a plan?"

"Hey," McCoy snapped, "I'm right here, you know."

"He does," the woman said.

"So, what is the problem?" Creed asked.

"If you must know," McCoy said in a voice dripping with sarcasm and alcohol, "I'm worried about falling on my ass."

Creed looked at the whore. "Get us some coffee."

"I'm fine," McCoy growled. "I've got this." He picked up the bottle of whiskey and watched in amazement as it slipped through his fingers and crashed to the floor at his feet. "Oops."

"Get the coffee," the Texan said.

The woman walked away while Creed sat at the table. He said, "I want a job. I heard you were hiring."

McCoy, who was still trying to work out how his bottle had ended up on the floor, looked at him and asked, "Who are you?"

"The name's Creed."

"You a Texan?"

"Yes, sir."

"Then go find a herd. That's right, waste of time

because there are no damned buyers."

"I heard you had a plan," Creed said again.

McCoy's nod was overly emphatic because of the amount of liquor he'd consumed. "I do. If the train and stock cars ever get here."

"You're going to need men to work with you. You got any?"

"Nope. Where's my bottle?"

Creed sighed. It was useless trying to conduct a conversation with McCoy while he was like this. He'd be better off to wait until the following morning.

The woman appeared with a coffee pot and two cups. When she placed them on the table, Creed thanked her, and she moved away. The Texan poured two cups and pushed one across the table.

"Here, drink this."

"What is it?"

"Coffee."

McCoy screwed up his face. "I got a bottle."

"You did until you dropped it," Creed reminded him. "Just drink the damned coffee."

If McCoy didn't sober up, the railway could kiss its investment goodbye, and that was something Creed wasn't prepared to let happen.

He sensed another presence in the room before turning to see Rio Wade standing just inside the doors. The hired killer briefly scanned the room, taking in the table with Creed seated opposite McCoy.

"I gotta go," McCoy grumbled.

Creed glanced at him, noticing the sudden pallor of his visage and realizing McCoy was trying to keep the contents of his stomach down. After lurching to his feet, knocking over his chair in the process, McCoy staggered toward the back of the saloon and went out through a rear door.

"Something I said?" Wade asked as he came up to the table.

Creed looked up at the gunman and shook his head. "Something he drank."

Wade gave a grunt that could have been a laugh. "Reckon we've all been there."

"You want to sit down?" the Texan asked.

Wade nodded. "Sure."

He picked up the chair and sat down, then pointed at McCoy's untouched cup of coffee and raised his eyebrows in an unspoken question. "Be my guest," Creed said.

Wade took a sip and placed it back on the scarred tabletop. He stared at Creed for a moment as though sizing the man up, then asked, "Why are you in town, Creed?"

"You know my name," Creed noted.

"I asked. Made it a point to after you shot the finger off one of my men."

Creed shrugged. "I did warn him."

"So I heard."

"He's got no one to blame but himself."

Wade drank more coffee, then said, "You didn't answer my question."

"I guess I never did," Creed allowed. "I'm just passing through, looking for work."

"You won't find any around here."

"You sound so sure," Creed said.

"Pretty much."

"I heard McCoy had a venture going."

"So did I," Wade said. "Personally, don't really see it working out, though."

"Maybe I'll find something else," Creed told him.

Wade shook his head. "Can't see where. No buyers means no cattle. No cattle means no work. Maybe you should try your luck elsewhere."

"You sound like you don't want me around, Wade."

"I'm impressed. You took the time to find out who *I* am."

"You ain't the only one who can ask questions."

"As I was saying, it might pay for you to look somewhere else for work. I don't see a future here."

Creed nodded. "I'll consider it."

Wade climbed to his feet. "You do that. Thanks for the coffee."

The Texan watched Wade leave. "Consider yourself warned," he muttered to himself as he removed his hand from the butt of his Colt.

* * *

The following day brought three things to Abilene: a locomotive, a Texas herd, and angry cowboys who couldn't cut loose because there were no buyers, which meant no wages.

The arrival of the Baldwin 4-4-0 locomotive with the two stock cars started the day out well for the hungover McCoy. It whistled as it came in, shattering the serenity of the morning. He hurried across to the siding just as it came to a halt. The engineer climbed down and just about had his arm wrenched from its socket, McCoy was shaking his hand so hard.

"Is it all right there, Mr. McCoy?" the mustachioed driver asked.

"Lance, you could leave it in the main street for all I care. I'm just happy to see you."

"You build us a track, and we'll do just that." Lance chortled.

They laughed together, and when the large fireman, Ernie, climbed down, he received the same reception.

Creed watched from a distance as the three men talked. He sensed a presence beside him and turned to see Liza standing there.

"Those boxes ain't strong enough to hold buffalo," the young woman said.

"No, I don't see as they are," Creed agreed.

"He'll have to reinforce them with some strong lumber," the cowboy named Hawk said as he joined them.

"I expect so."

"You get that job?" Liza asked Creed.

Creed remembered their conversation the previous evening. "Not yet. Might be a good time now to ask, though."

He walked over to where the three men were still talking. The trio broke up and McCoy stared at the Texan, wracking his brain to work out where he'd seen him before.

"Last night," Creed said, helping him out.

McCoy winced. "Oh, yes. Not my best performance."

"I'm after a job. Heard you had one going."

"I've got more than one if you're interested?"

Creed nodded. "Good—"

The morning was split by the banshee howl of a lone rider galloping along the street, right up to where the train was stopped. He took one look at the stock cars and said loudly, "You'll need more than two of them things for what we got."

The Texas drawl was unmistakable. "Which herd?" McCoy asked.

"Triangle T," the cowboy said. "We got three thousand of the orneriest critters you ever saw."

McCoy said, "Well, shoot, bring them on in. Let your boss know the yards are waiting."

"I'll sure do that, mister," the cowboy said gleefully, then wheeled his horse around and took off, the animal's hooves kicking up dust as it went.

Creed looked at McCoy, whose face suddenly turned down. He said to the Texan, "I don't know what to do. There's not a buyer this side of Chicago who'll come here."

"You give me a job, and I'll get you a buyer," Creed said. "Let me ramrod this venture you've got going."

"You get me a buyer, and I'll do just that," McCoy told him. "But one buyer won't be enough."

"It'll be a start."

"Yes, it will."

"There's one more thing. You let me do the hiring and firing."

"Wait just a minute—" McCoy started.

"Take it or leave it. Then you can find yourself a buyer."

"All right, all right. But you better be able to find

a buyer, or Abilene will be overrun by a mob baying for blood. Mine."

Creed's face was serious as he nodded. "I'll get you a buyer."

The Texan turned and walked away. When he reached the spot where Hawk and Liza were still standing, he stopped and asked, "You two want some work?"

"You got a job?" Liza asked.

Creed nodded. "Ramrodding the man's foolishness."

"What did you have in mind?" Hawk asked.

"You think you can fix one of those stock cars up?"

"I can do that."

"That's your first job. Work out what you need and go see McCoy. Tell him you're working for me."

"What about me?" Liza asked.

"We'll need a small remuda," Creed told her. "The people I hire will have their own broncs, but we'll need more."

"I'll see what I can find. What'll I do for money?"

"See McCoy. Don't let anyone buffalo you."

"Don't worry, I won't."

He looked at her and nodded, smiling faintly as he said, "I didn't really figure you would."

* * *

Creed went to the telegraph office and sent a wire to Faraday. He received one back two hours later, telling him he'd do what he could. A second one followed an hour later, saying that there would be a buyer on a train in two days.

The Texan was surprised by the swiftness of things being put into place and knew Faraday had pulled a few strings to make it happen. Creed then went and found McCoy, who was overseeing the start of the strengthening of the stock car.

"I see you've already started," Creed said.

"Yes," replied McCoy. "The man you hired seems to know what he's doing."

"I had a feeling he would," the Texan said.

"The girl, too. She's already started bringing in some horses."

Creed nodded.

"How did you do with a buyer?" McCoy asked tentatively.

"Be here in a couple of days," Creed informed him.

Shaking his head in disbelief, McCoy said, "I didn't think you could do it."

"That was the easy part. You're going to have to convince the trail boss of the herd not to leave."

"I know. I'm not looking forward to that part."

* * *

"I got a message here from the telegrapher," Kent said, passing the piece of paper to Wade as he sat in the Longhorn Saloon.

Rio opened it and read through the scrawl, then folded it and tucked it away. "Go back and tell him to send the same message to Mr. Miles. And tell him to mention the herd that's arriving today. Also, tell him to find out who that Faraday fella is."

The herd and now a buyer coming on the train in

a couple of days, Wade thought. This wasn't good. He gathered the others around him and said, "I want you men to burn that stock car tonight."

"You don't think that idiot idea of McCoy's could actually work, do you, Rio?" Slim asked.

"Can't take the chance that it will," Wade said. "I have a feeling Mr. Miles will be here tomorrow once he hears what's happening."

* * *

"What the hell do you mean, there's no damn buyers here?" the trail boss roared.

"There's no buyer. They all up and left after the Kelly herd got hit," McCoy explained. "Their excuse was Texas Fever."

"There's no blamed Texas Fever on these cows, damn it," Clyde Reynolds snarled.

"I told them that, and they still wouldn't stay."

"I wish I'd have knowed this before. I'd've gone to Ellsworth."

"No," McCoy said urgently. "That's what he wants."

"Who?"

"Hank Miles. He wants the herds to go there so he can buy them cheap and sell them to buyers for a better price. By doing that, you lose out."

"Well, tell me then, McCoy, what do I do now?" Reynolds demanded.

"I have a buyer coming the day after tomorrow. If you want, hold the herd outside of Abilene and fatten them on the grass."

"What am I gonna tell my hands? Sorry, I can't pay you yet? They'll turn this town upside down."

Creed stood to one side, watching this confrontation. He suggested, "How about if McCoy gives you some of his own money to tide them over for a couple of days?"

"What?" McCoy asked, staring at him in surprise.

Reynolds rubbed his chin and frowned in thought. "Hmm, might work," the trail boss said.

McCoy swallowed, heaved a sigh of acceptance, and said, "Good, tell your boys to be over at the Drover's Cottage in an hour."

"Fine, I'll do that."

Reynolds left, and McCoy wheeled on the Texan. "What the hell did you just do?"

"I just saved you from getting your town wrecked."

"Where am I supposed to get the money I just promised him?" McCoy demanded.

"I didn't give him a total," Creed pointed out. "Give them ten bucks each and arrange for some free alcohol at the Cottage."

"You'll break me, damn it."

"You'll be broker still if they take that herd to Ellsworth."

McCoy shook his head and growled, "I hope this works."

* * *

"Damn it," Miles exclaimed when he saw the wire. "What the hell does he hope to achieve?"

He crumpled the piece of paper and dropped it

on his desk. This little venture of McCoy's had to be stopped, and the buyer couldn't be allowed to get his hands on that herd. There was only one thing to do.

Miles needed to go to Abilene and buy the herd right out from under McCoy.

Chapter 6

The Drover's Cottage saloon was jumping that evening. It was the first time in a while. Cowboys were lined up at the bar getting drunk, while others sat at tables with a bottle in the middle of the battered surface for them to share.

A loud female yelp signaled that the cowboys weren't the only ones having fun. McCoy could see money slipping through his fingers and felt like crying. Clyde Reynolds walked up to his table and said, "What kind of place is this? You only got three girls."

"Send your boys across the tracks about a mile and they'll find what they need. There's some canvas tents out there with whores who'll take care of their needs."

Reynolds raised his eyebrows. "A mile? What kind of town has prostitutes a mile outside the city limits?"

"This one. Besides, they might be sober enough to enjoy themselves by the time they get there."

Reynolds chuckled. "They *are* a little drunk."

"It'll be worse tomorrow night," McCoy told him.

Reynolds frowned. "Hmm. Yeah, when Bernie Warriner gets in with his crew. I hope you got spare furniture somewhere. They're a wild bunch. They took a herd up the Shawnee a while back and just about wrecked Sedalia."

Bernie Warriner owned and trail-bossed his own cattle from his Broken W ranch. McCoy nodded glumly and said, "I know, I was there. I got a couple scatterguns behind the bar. Any of your hands looking to earn a few extra dollars?"

"I'll ask around."

"Thanks."

McCoy saw Creed enter the bar and raised his hand to get the Texan's attention. Creed made his way over to the table. As he sat down, he said, "Busy night."

"Yes, and I'm not getting a damned cent out of it."

"Once the buyer arrives, you'll be fine."

"Listen," said Reynolds. "I appreciate what you're doing for my boys. If you want to keep a tally, once we sell the herd, I'll pay you back what you advanced us."

Creed smiled. "See, it all worked out."

"How's the stock car coming along?" McCoy asked.

"It'll be ready tomorrow. The other will be fine for the horses."

"You hired anyone else yet?"

"Plenty of cowboys in here. I figured to wait until they're sober and see who jumps aboard."

Reynolds laughed and slapped the table hard enough for the glasses to jump. "If I ever seen a man with a bull by the tail, you would be it. Trying to rope growed buffalo and put them on a train. That is some fool notion you got there, McCoy."

"I need something to bring the buyers back."

The trail boss turned his gaze on Creed. "And you a Texan. I'd thought for sure you'd have more sense at least."

"I like a challenge." Creed smiled. "Makes life interesting."

"Hell. I tell you what, I'll put the word out with my boys, and if any of them want to help, I won't stop them. But this is still a damned foolish idea."

"Fire!" a voice yelled. "There's a fire over at the siding."

Creed came to his feet, his chair scraping the floorboards as it was pushed back. He didn't have to see the blaze to know what it was. He ran toward the door, followed by McCoy.

From outside the saloon, he could see the orange flames leaping and lighting the night. The stock car was well ablaze, and there would be no saving it.

McCoy spewed and sputtered curses while he and Creed trotted toward the siding. Creed stopped forty yards short of the burning car, its heat reaching out to him. The shorter-legged McCoy caught up and stumbled to a halt beside him.

"Well, that is that," McCoy declared in a tone of utter disgust.

"The hell it is," Creed growled. "Tomorrow, I'm going to get you another stock car. I'll be back the day after that."

McCoy turned to face him, confusion evident on his face. "How? Who the hell are you, Creed? You sure aren't a cowhand. You conjured up a buyer out of thin air. Now you say you can somehow get another stock car just like that? What aren't you telling me?"

Before Creed could reply, Liza Kelly and Jack Hawk hurried up, drawn by the commotion like many of the other folks in Abilene.

"Oh, no," Liza said as she and Hawk stopped beside Creed and McCoy. "Who did this?"

"Give you one guess," Creed commented dryly.

"Rio Wade?"

"That would be my guess."

"What do we do now?" Liza asked.

McCoy said, "Creed says he can get a stock car. He's leaving in the morning."

"How?"

"That's what I just asked him."

There was a crunching sound as the frame of the stock car gave way and its roof collapsed. Creed said, "All right, I'll give you some answers, but not here."

"Come over to my office in the Drover's," McCoy said. "We can talk there."

They walked away from the burning mess and through the crowd that had gathered when the call went out to watch the spectacle. Once inside, they stopped.

Standing at the bar were Rio Wade and his friends, joking and laughing.

Wade saw them and asked, "You look like you lost something. Have a fire?"

McCoy took a step forward, bristling with anger, but Creed stopped him.

"Not now, Joe," he said, reining in his own temper. It wasn't an easy thing to do.

"You better listen to the saddle tramp, Joe." Wade grinned.

Creed could feel eyes on him, but he wasn't about to take his own off the killer in front of him. "I'm not a saddle tramp, Wade. I work for the Faraday Security Agency. We take care of railways."

Wade looked surprised by that revelation, but he shrugged it off and said, "I couldn't work out what your game was, but it doesn't matter." The killer straightened up. "Maybe it's time for you to go."

"You going to make me?"

Wade pulled back his coat flap to reveal the butt of his six-gun. "Maybe."

Creed shook his head. "I'm not going to kill you, Wade. Maybe just whale the tar out of you, Texas-style."

Wade smirked. "Just you and me?"

"Sure, why not?"

Wade started to remove his coat. Creed followed suit and took off his own jacket, followed by his Colt. He coiled the gunbelt and handed it to McCoy. "Hold that for me."

He saw the look in Liza Kelly's eyes and added, "Don't worry about me. I'm from Texas like you, remember? Besides, after I'm done here, I'm going to buy you supper."

This declaration brought a smile to her lips. "You are, are you?"

"Is there a reason why you think I can't?"

"Just get through this fight first, and we'll see."

The gunman gave Creed a wicked grin as the Texan turned to face him. "I guess we'll find out what you're made of, huh?"

The two closed the distance between them, and Wade's left streaked forward like the strike of a rattler. Creed was expecting it and moved his head, so the blow missed. Creed countered with a right fist that connected solidly with Wade's jaw, rocking his head back. The killer took a couple of steps back before he dropped his head and charged.

Wade's shoulder drove into Creed's middle and sent him back against the solid bar. The Texan grunted from the pain that ripped through his back from the edge of the counter.

Creed locked both his hands together and brought them down on the back of Wade's neck. The man lurched back, and the Texan hit him on the jaw.

Wade staggered back some more, and Creed followed him. He hit him again, sending the killer back even farther. His feet got tangled with a chair, and the wood splintered as he crashed onto it.

Wade climbed to his feet and wiped at a thin line of blood running from the corner of his mouth. He glanced briefly at the back of his hand and spat blood on the floor at his feet. With a growl from deep inside him, Wade flexed his fingers and walked forward.

Creed hit him, but the blow seemed to do nothing. It was as though Wade suddenly felt no pain. The Texan hit him again with the same result. Going for a third punch, he was stunned when Wade let go with a looping right that caught Creed on the lips, mashing them against his teeth and splitting the fleshy bottom one.

Now they were both bleeding.

The Texan backed away, shaking his head to clear the cobwebs. "Is that all you got?" he managed to taunt Wade.

A guttural growl signaled another attack from the gunman, who took two steps forward and walked into a straight right that stopped him in his tracks.

McCoy saw it happen and winced. There was a lot of power in the punch, so he was surprised Wade was still standing.

Creed drew on his inner strength and followed the blow with three more in quick succession. Two rights and a left struck home with enough power to put Wade on his heels and then dump him on the floor.

"You had enough?" Creed asked, sucking in a lungful of air.

"I'm only just getting started," Wade snarled as he regained his feet.

The words had barely left his mouth when Creed hit him again, putting Wade back where he'd come from. This time the killer was less enthusiastic about hauling himself to his feet. Creed stood over him and said, "This is over. How about you take your men and leave town? You ain't wanted here, Wade."

Wade climbed to his feet and spat on the floor. "This is a long way from over." He turned to his men and rasped, "Come on, we're leaving."

With sullen looks, they all left the saloon.

Once they were gone, McCoy said to Creed, "You know things just got worse, don't you?"

Creed took his bandanna from his pocket, dabbed his bloody lips, and grimaced. "Maybe, but at least things are out in the open now."

"You really a Faraday man?"

Creed nodded and told them the story of why he was there. McCoy gave a low whistle. "That explains why you can get things done."

"I'm sorry I didn't say anything sooner, but I wanted to get the lay of the land first."

"The stock car—where are you going to get it from?" Hawk asked.

Creed smiled despite the blood on his lips. "I'm going to steal it."

* * *

"Do you really think you can pull it off?" Liza asked Creed across the table where their supper sat.

He nodded. "Should be simple enough. Ride in on the locomotive, hitch it up, and bring it back."

"But Ellsworth? That's not just poking the bear. More like slapping it on the rump and waving a red rag at it when it turns around."

Creed's grin grew wider. "I never thought of it that way. I like the way you think."

It took a few moments before Liza realized she was staring at him. Her gaze dropped, and her face colored.

"Don't be embarrassed. I like looking at your eyes," he told her.

Liza's color deepened. "You just made it worse."

"I'm sorry. I figure that if some things don't get said, later on, it might be too late."

"Is that how you excuse being so forward?"

"Yes, did it work?"

Liza smiled. "I'll let you know."

They ate their meals, then Creed paid the check and escorted Liza outside into the cool night air. A cloudless sky created an inky backdrop for the belt of stars winking and sparkling like diamonds.

"Would it be too forward of me to ask to escort you back to your hotel?"

"Damn it, Creed, you know damn well I'm staying at the Cottage," Liza snapped.

He chuckled. "Sure, I do."

"Then take me there."

"With pleasure."

"And get that damn grin off your face, or I won't let you kiss me goodnight."

"I get a kiss, do I?"

"I didn't say that."

He offered her his arm, and they began walking toward the Drover's Cottage. "What do you plan on doing, Liza?" Creed asked.

"I have a ranch in Texas to run," she replied.

"What about the money you've lost? Won't that make it hard?"

"At first, but we'll scrape through. We always do."

With no warning, a shot blasted somewhere in the night. The bullet whipped between the two of them just above shoulder height, so close Creed heard it sizzle through the air. A couple of inches either way, and it would have been disastrous.

"Get down!" Creed said as he pushed Liza to the street. A second bullet dug into the earth not far from where they crouched.

Creed drew his Colt and thumbed back the hammer. The third shot from the bushwhacker missed, too, but it gave Creed a chance to see the muzzle flash from across the way, near the stockyards. The would-be killer was determined, but not enough to come closer to make sure of his kill.

Creed triggered a pair of swift shots in return and told Liza, "Find some cover!"

He fired two more shots as she came to her feet and started to run toward the Cottage.

The Texan, on the other hand, charged toward the stockyards. His shoulder hit one of the wooden rails as a bullet chewed splinters from it. Creed snapped off another shot in the bushwhacker's direction before reloading.

When the man fired next, he'd shifted, but his muzzle flashes indicated the new position. Creed moved to his right with the hammer on his Colt eared back, weapon ready to fire once more.

The shooter fired again, the crack of the rifle loud in the night air. The bullet flew wide, but it told Creed where the would-be killer was. His gun barked three times, and he was rewarded with the sound of a yelp from across the open yard. Creed squeezed between the rails and ran across the pen, firing once more as he went. When he reached the far side, he leaped at the fence, scrambled over the top rail, and dropped to the ground on the other side.

The Texan remained in a crouch, listening for anything that might indicate the position of the ambusher. The sound of retreating footsteps reached his ears. The bushwhacker was getting away.

Creed came to his feet and holstered the Colt. He muttered an inaudible curse and turned to climb the fence behind him. Whoever it was—and he had a fair idea—would more than likely try again, and he might not be so lucky next time.

Chapter 7

Hank Miles stepped down from his personal train the following morning. His business dealings had made him a wealthy man, and this was one of the benefits of it. He was able to travel wherever and whenever he liked as long as the steel rails went there.

Despite his wealth, Miles was prepared to get down in the mud and fight if he had to, but he preferred to leave that to others unless his personal touch was necessary.

The issue in Abilene was getting to that point pretty fast.

"Howdy, Mr. Miles," Wade greeted him as his polished shoes hit the gravel beside his lavish rail car.

Miles stared at his troubleshooter and nodded. "What happened to you, Rio?"

"Nothing I can't handle," Wade replied.

"I see," Wade said. He looked at the cloudless sky. The sun was already making the morning hot. "Well, let's go and find this trail boss and buy his herd."

"If you'd let me shoot McCoy, Mr. Miles, it would

save you a lot of problems."

"I might have entertained the idea if we didn't have the added complication of the man from the Faraday agency," Miles replied. "But we'll have to tread carefully for a while when it comes to Joseph McCoy."

"Yes, sir," Wade said with reluctant acceptance. "I've got a horse waiting for you."

* * *

"So that's Miles, huh?" Creed inquired as he and McCoy watched the man and his hired guns ride out of town.

"That's him. Damned son of a bitch if there was ever one."

"Gets around in style," Creed observed.

"Yes, on blood money and the backs of others."

"You figure he's going to see Reynolds to make an offer on the herd?"

"Without a doubt. I'd say he's heard of the buyer we've got coming in. The same way he heard about you being a Faraday man."

Creed gave him a puzzled look.

"The telegrapher we have is a little unscrupulous," McCoy informed him.

"Why don't you get rid of him?"

"He's the only one around who can do the damned job."

"Watch your back while I'm gone," Creed told him.

"Yes, sir, I will. Don't you worry none about that."

As the riders disappeared, Lance and Ernie, the

engineer and the fireman who had brought the train to Abilene, walked up. Lance looked at Creed and said, "We're ready when you are, Mr. Creed."

"All right, then, let's go steal a stock car."

"Good luck," said McCoy.

"We'll be back before dark," Creed promised.

* * *

"Are you Reynolds?" Miles asked the trail boss when they rode up to the camp outside of town.

Most of the hands were still in town, but a couple of them, along with Reynolds, had stayed with the cattle the night before. The trail boss knew the only way to keep them all happy was to work the men in shifts, so that was what he did.

"I am," Reynolds said.

"Good. I'm Hank Miles. I'm here to buy your herd."

"Are you now?" Reynolds replied.

"I'll give you fifteen dollars a head. All you have to do is deliver them to Ellsworth."

The trail boss stared at Miles for a long minute to see if the man was joking. Apparently, he wasn't. "Why would I do that when there's a railhead right here?"

"Because I'm offering to pay you good money for your cattle," Miles told him.

"Fifteen dollars a head is hardly good money, Miles," Reynolds pointed out. "I think I'll wait for the buyer that McCoy has coming in."

"This is my first and best offer, Reynolds," Miles warned him. "If I have to make a second, it won't be so generous."

"We're done here. The buyer will arrive tomorrow. I guess I'll be selling the herd to him."

"Boss," Wade said, drawing Miles' attention.

Miles glared at him, his anger bubbling just below the surface. "What?"

"Over there," Wade said, looking to the south.

Miles' eyes followed the direction of his gaze, and he saw the smudge of dust on the horizon. "Another herd?"

"That'll be the Broken W herd," Reynolds divulged. "Bernie Warriner and his crew. You could always try him."

"Come on, Rio," Miles snapped. "Let's go and meet Mr. Warriner. We're done here for the moment."

* * *

The Broken W herd was strung out in a long line, allowed to pick its way across the landscape in no hurry like a winding serpent sunbaking. The riders found Bernie Warriner on point with his ramrod, a mountain of a man with a bushy black beard.

Warriner was the opposite. He was a nuggety compact gent with a thorny disposition. "What do you want?" he growled at the riders.

"I'm here to buy your herd, Warriner," Miles told him.

"Who are you?"

"Hank Miles."

"What are you offering?"

"Fifteen dollars a head."

Warriner nodded. "I heard of you, Miles. Just wanted to make sure you were the right one. You've wasted your time riding out here. I'll wait to talk to the buyer McCoy has coming in."

"Mister—"

"Conversation's over, Miles. I got work to do."

The trail boss and the ramrod rode away, leaving Miles seething inside. Wade asked, "What do you want to do, boss?"

Miles glared after the two men. "We try a little persuasion."

* * *

When the Baldwin locomotive arrived in Ellsworth, a herd was being loaded onto a string of stock cars. It was nothing out of the ordinary for a railhead, but it did catch Creed's interest. When the engine stopped, he said to Lance, "Locate a car. I'm going over to the yards to check something out."

The cows were Texas animals and fine-looking beasts. It looked as though, in preparation for the trip east, they'd been fattened on the grass outside of town. Creed watched them being loaded, some moving up easily, others more stubborn. However, the yard hands had more than enough experience to deal with the obnoxious animals, and soon another car was loaded.

Creed spotted a brindle beast with an odd-looking brand, a W between two lines—except one of the lines was crooked. Not by much, just a little. Then he saw another. And a third.

He called out to one of the loaders, "What brand?"

"Wilson River."

"Texas?"

"Sure."

Creed climbed up onto the rail and watched some more. He sat there for an hour and counted a further fifty animals with irregular brands. Lance found him there and said, "We got a car."

"Unhitch it."

"What?" the engineer asked incredulously.

"I've got something else for you to hook up to."

Lance shook his head. "All right then, you're the boss. Although you could have told me about it before we got it done."

Creed ignored him and called to one of the yard hands who was about to run the last cow onto the final stock car, "Hold that steer there."

The man looked at him curiously. "What for?"

"Because I said so."

Creed climbed down into the yard to get a closer look at the brand, but the animal wouldn't keep still. He said to the cowboy, "You got a butcher in town?"

"Yeah, sure."

"You'd best get him."

"Why?" the man demanded.

Creed drew his Colt and shot the steer in one swift movement. The animal dropped to its belly, spasmed, and rolled onto its side.

"Go and get him."

"Who the hell do you think you are, mister?"

Creed showed him his Faraday badge. "You going to go fetch that butcher or not?"

While the man was gone, others gathered around, staring at the dead animal and giving Creed accusatory glares. Finally, the man appeared with the butcher, who wore a blood-stained apron.

"You want me, mister?" he growled. "I was busy, you know. Cutting up a forequarter. Meat don't keep for very long when it's out."

"That's fine. After you do what I want you to, you can have this animal free of charge."

"Just wait a damned minute, stranger," the cowboy snarled.

Creed ignored him and said to the butcher, "Skin the brand off this animal for me. Do it good, or I'm going to have to keep shooting cows until you get it right. I don't want to do that."

With practiced ease, the butcher had the brand off within minutes. He handed the flap of hide to Creed, who examined it, then lifted the hide to his nose and smelled it. The odor of scorched hair lingered; the brand had been altered recently. He turned the flap back over, revealing the older markings of the original brand. The steer had belonged to the Lazy K herd.

Creed turned to the cowboy. "Who's in charge?"

"I am," a voice from behind the Texan said.

Creed turned and saw a burly man with shaggy brown hair down to his collar. "Who are you?"

"Frost," the man replied curtly. "I'm in charge of shipping for Mr. Miles."

"You know these cattle aren't what they seem to be?"

The man shook his head. "Nope."

"I believe they belong to a herd that was rustled—"

"Wouldn't know a thing about that," Frost growled. "Got a bill of sale right here."

"Let me have a look."

"Nope. It ain't got nothin' to do with you."

Creed nodded. "Fine. Here's what's going to happen. I'm going to hook a locomotive up to these cars, and I'm taking them with me. All of these cows are going to the rightful owner."

"You can't do that," Frost exclaimed. "Mr. Miles paid good money—"

"I don't believe that for a minute," Creed said, cutting him off. "Even if he did, I don't much care. He should be more careful about who he buys them from."

"You won't get away with this," Frost blustered.

"I do believe I will," Creed said.

An hour later, the cars were hooked up and ready to roll out of Ellsworth.

* * *

When the news came, Miles was sitting in the Longhorn Saloon with Rio Wade, contemplating his next move. He looked at the piece of paper the telegrapher had given him and read it twice, then placed it down upon the table. He drew in a deep breath and let it out in a hiss that sounded like steam escaping from a boiler.

"Problem, Mr. Miles?" Wade asked his boss.

Miles said nothing, just gestured for Wade to read the message for himself. Rio reached for the slip of paper, scanned the words before staring dumbly at his boss.

"I wasn't expecting that," Wade said. "What the hell was he doing in Ellsworth anyhow?"

"Those cows are worth sixty thousand dollars to me, damn it," Miles said in a low voice. "I'm not going to let them go without a fight."

"Just tell us what you want done, Mr. Miles, and we'll do it."

"You already have something to do for me. I'll deal with this myself."

* * *

The train rolled into Abilene late that afternoon, about thirty minutes before dark. It lined up with the yards so the cows could be unloaded and watered, ready for the buyer coming to Abilene in a day or so to look them over.

As soon as McCoy heard about the train, he made his way to the yards. Creed was unloading the beasts when he arrived. "What's all this?" McCoy asked.

"That's the Lazy K herd."

McCoy stared at him. "What?"

"I found them in Ellsworth," the Texan explained. "They were being loaded when I got there. I noticed a lot of funny brands, and on closer inspection, I discovered someone had altered them." Creed shrugged. "So I took them."

"I can guess what will happen next," McCoy said warily. "I'm assuming Miles is tied up in this somewhere."

"His stock boss told me he had a bill of sale for them."

"But you took them anyway."

"Yep."

"I thought you were only going for a car, not a herd," Liza Kelly said as she and Hawk walked up.

Creed turned to face her and said, "While it's still daylight, I want you to look over the herd, Liza, and tell me if you recognize any of them."

"What?" she asked, confused.

"I'm reasonably sure this is your herd, although the brands have been altered. Sorry I had to shoot one to prove it."

Liza was stunned. "This is my herd?"

"I think so, yes."

Suddenly she threw her arms around him and kissed him on the lips. It was hard and passionate and surprising. She drew back and said, "I'm sorry, but—"

"Nothing to apologize for," Creed told her with a smile. "Let's just make sure they're yours."

"They're mine, not hers," a new voice said.

Creed turned to face Hank Miles. The man continued as he stalked toward them, "I have a bill of sale, damn it."

"That's what your man claimed when I took the cattle," Creed said.

Miles' eyes narrowed. "We hang rustlers around here, Creed."

"Take it up with the person who sold you stolen cattle," the Texan told him. "They belong to Miss Kelly."

Miles shook his head. He dug into his pocket and

held out a piece of paper. He held it out for Creed to read. "I heard about what happened and got in touch with a friend who is a friend of the governor."

Creed read the telegram and looked at Miles once he'd finished it. "This isn't right," Creed said.

"The bill of sale and that note from the governor says it is."

"I guess he's got an election coming up," Creed said. "Must need money."

"I'll be taking the telegram back if you don't mind?"

Before he could hand it over, Liza snatched it out of Creed's hand. She started to read, and the further she got, the wider her eyes grew.

"This can't be."

"Afraid it is, Miss Kelly." Miles smirked in his triumph. "I bought that herd fair and square."

"From the Wilson River ranch?" Creed said.

"That's right."

"Ain't no Wilson River ranch," Hawk said.

"Not what I was told. Now, if you don't mind, you can put my cattle back on the train so they can go to market."

"Do it yourself," Creed said.

* * *

"Thank you for trying," Liza said to Creed as they stood outside the Cottage.

He reached out and grasped her hand and said, "I'm not done yet. I figured something out."

"They had to unload all the cattle because Lance

refused to let them use his locomotive to ship them. Hawk is working on one car he managed to put aside."

Creed nodded. "I sent word to my boss in Washington. I'm hoping he might be able to do something."

"You have to stop, John," she said. "He's got us beat."

"Not yet, he hasn't," Creed growled. "Not by a long sight."

The sound of a gunshot split the early evening and caused Liza to jump toward him. Creed wrapped his arms around her protectively and said, "It's all right, it wasn't close."

Liza looked up into his eyes, and instead of stepping back, she pressed against him. "John—"

The moment was interrupted by urgent shouts of alarm. He looked at her and said, "I have to go."

Liza took a step back and said, "Can we finish this later?"

"Sure," Creed responded with a smile.

"Then you'd better go."

Creed hurried toward the trouble, and when he arrived, the first words he heard clearly were, "They shot Reynolds."

Creed pushed through the throng to where the man lay on the ground. "Did anyone see what happened?"

When no one spoke up, Creed knelt to check the trail boss. As he expected, Reynolds was dead. Creed got back to his feet and asked himself why someone would want Reynolds dead.

Creed looked around. "Who here is from Reynolds' crew?"

Most of the cowboys were.

"Can any of you tell me—"

"Don't you have the law here?" one of them broke in to demand angrily.

"Not currently," McCoy said as he walked out of the darkness. "We're working on it."

"Then we'll do the job ourselves," the man snapped and drew his gun to make a point.

"Just hold up," McCoy said. "Just because we have no law don't mean we ain't civilized. Any of you hands think you can form some kind of vigilance committee, think again."

Creed tried again. "Did he have trouble with anyone?"

"No," said one of the men. "He was out at the herd most of the time. Although we did get visitors earlier today."

"Who?" asked Creed.

"That Miles *hombre*. He came out to offer to buy the herd."

Creed remembered seeing Miles and Wade ride out of town. "What happened?"

"The boss told him no."

"What was he offering?"

"Fifteen dollars a head. He also told him the price from here on would only go down."

Creed nodded. "You'd better get the body off the street."

Reynolds was taken away, and the Texan turned to McCoy. "You thinking what I am?"

"If you're thinking Miles had Reynolds killed, then yeah, I'm thinking the same thing," McCoy said. "Poor *hombre* signed his own death warrant when he turned down Miles' offer."

"Looks like Mile is getting desperate."

"Desperate enough to steal a herd and kill a passel of people?"

"The buyer should be here tomorrow," Creed pointed out. "Hawk will work on the stock car we'll take, and we should be ready to go the day after."

"Good. I received word today that there are more herds on the trail headed north. We need to get this done to get the buyers here."

"We will."

With a glum look on his face, McCoy said, "I hope you're right, Creed. If you're not, Abilene is finished."

Chapter 8

Rudy Banks loved his work, and the small house on the outskirts of Kansas City provided him with a sanctuary in which to carry it out in relative comfort. The sleeves of his white shirt were rolled up past his elbows, and there was a thin sheen of sweat on his brow that reflected the orange lantern light whenever he turned his head.

Rubbing his hawklike nose, he sniffed audibly. He gave a grunt as he moved across to the table in search of a new tool to use.

"Knife? Thin sliver of wood? Fingernail pullers? Bone saw? Scalpel? I'm not sure." He turned to face the bloody man tied to the chair with a gag forced into his mouth. "I'm not sure, Mr. Chapple. What do you think?"

The man's muffled pleas were choked off by the disgusting cloth, but his partially closed eyes said it all. Banks cocked his head to one side. "What was that?"

More muffled grunts.

Banks stepped over to the man and pulled the rag out of Chapple's mouth. "Please speak clearly, man. Say again?"

"Pl...please. Don't do this."

"Maybe you should have thought about the consequences of your actions before you started sleeping with Michael Guilfoyle's wife. Yes?"

"It wasn't my fault," he blurted. "She seduced me."

"Mr. Guilfoyle is aware of that," Banks informed him. "But still, it does not alter the fact that you slept with his wife on more than one occasion."

"What?"

"Oh, didn't I tell you? Charlotte and I had an in-depth conversation the other evening. She was quite talkative toward the end."

"Oh, Go—"

His last word was cut off as Banks stuffed the rag back into Chapple's mouth. Banks returned to the table, searching through his tools once more. He picked up a long, thin, needle-sharp piece of metal and held it up in front of his face. "I think we'll start with the eyes."

* * *

"Mr. Banks?" the hotel clerk called after the killer as he started up the stairs of the hotel to the second-floor landing, holding a small valise.

Banks turned around and stared at the clerk, annoyed at the inconvenience. "What is it?"

"There was a telegram came for you late this afternoon, sir. I have it right here."

With a loud sigh, Banks descended the few steps and went across the dimly lit foyer to the hardwood counter where the clerk waited, holding the telegram in his right hand. The killer took it and said, "Thank you."

"Did you hurt yourself, sir?" the clerk asked.

Banks frowned. "Why would you ask that?"

"Oh, I saw a little blood on your hand."

Banks looked at the hand with the telegram in it and saw what the clerk was talking about. He smiled and said, "That? Just a scratch. Caught it on a hitch rail earlier when I was crossing the street."

"Need to be more careful, sir."

"You're right."

Banks moved away from the counter to where one of the wall lamps provided sufficient illumination for him to read the message. When he was finished, he asked the clerk, "What time does the next train for Abilene come through?"

The clerk glanced at his pocket watch. "Two in the morning."

"Thank you."

Banks went upstairs and prepared to leave, after which he lay back on his bed and waited for the train with a serene smile on his face.

* * *

The train arrived an hour late, not that it worried Banks. He was in no rush to get where he was going. The train wheezed to a stop, and a baggage attendant climbed down from the rear car and walked toward him.

"Just the one bag, sir?" he asked Banks.

"Yes, thank you."

The man took it, and the killer climbed into the first of the two coach cars. He stopped inside the door and looked down the aisle. There were few passengers, and most seemed to be sleeping. Coming toward him through the darkened coach was a conductor.

"Do you have a ticket, sir?"

Banks nodded and showed him. The conductor nodded and said, "Take a seat wherever you like, sir. Have a pleasant journey."

"Before you go," Banks said, "I'm looking for a passenger named Tolliver. He's a cattle buyer headed to Abilene. I was told he'd be on the train."

The conductor frowned. "Not heard the name, sir. The only cattle buyer we have on board is Mr. Hammond. He's in the next car back. Are you sure you were given the right name?"

"Oh, dear," Banks said in a worried tone. "Now I'm not sure. In the next car, you said?"

"Yes, sir. In the fourth row on the left side. He's most likely asleep now, though."

Banks nodded. "Yes, I'll leave it until the morning and catch him then."

"Yes, sir, probably best."

* * *

An hour later, after everyone had settled once more and the carriage's motions had rocked the passengers back to sleep, one man rose from his seat and made his way to the second car. As expected, it was dark, the only light provided by the moon in the clear sky as it flooded through the windows.

Banks counted the rows and found the man he was looking for seated by himself. He was asleep, his head dropped forward and resting on his chest. Even better, the seat behind him was vacant.

The killer slipped into it and leaned back against the rest. He waited and watched until he was certain the car was still quiet before taking out the needle-thin, sharp-pointed probe. Banks then leaned forward, and in two swift movements, clamped his hand over the man's mouth and inserted the probe under the base of his skull into his brain. The man stiffened and went still.

His work complete, Banks left the carriage quietly and went back to his seat.

The following morning, the conductor asked him if he'd caught up with Hammond. Banks shook his head. "No, I overslept a little. I'll wait until we disembark when we reach Abilene."

* * *

McCoy and Creed watched as the passengers left the train under an early morning Kansas sun. Three women and four men. Not one of them was the cattle buyer.

The Texan walked over to the conductor. "Was there a cattle buyer on the train meant to disembark here?"

The man nodded. "Sure, his name is Hammond. Didn't he get off?"

"I don't think so."

"He was asleep in the second car," the conductor said.

"You mind if I take a look?" Creed asked.

"Well, I—"

Creed showed him his badge.

"I guess it'll be fine. Come with me."

Creed followed the conductor onto the train and along the aisle to the seat where Hammond still sat, head down on his chest. The Texan needed only one look to tell him the man was dead.

"Damn it," Creed said softly.

"Why, he's dead," the conductor said in surprise and horror.

"Yes, sir. He is that."

"But why? How..."

"I intend to find out."

Creed started to walk away, and the conductor called after him, "Hey, what am I supposed to do with him?"

"I'll have someone take care of it."

"But the train needs to leave," the man protested.

"It'll just have to wait."

When Creed swung down from the railroad coach, McCoy could see that something was wrong. "Well? Where is he?"

"He's on the train, dead."

"What?"

"You heard me. He's dead."

"How?"

Creed shook his head. "I have no idea. Do you have a doctor in town?"

McCoy said, "Not a proper one. We have a fellow who used to be a surgeon's aide in the war."

"Get him. I want to know what this man died from."

* * *

Miles studied the small man standing before him in his room at the Longhorn and said, "You're Banks?"

"I am."

"I gather by your presence that your job is done?"

"You gather right," the killer said.

Wade studied the man and thought to himself that Banks didn't look anything like the stories suggested. Banks could feel the gunman's eyes and turned his head. "Believe me, I can kill you before you even know about it."

The hired gun gave the killer his coldest smile and replied, "Maybe we'll find out one day."

"Perhaps we will."

"If you two are quite finished, I have another job for you, Banks," Miles said.

"What might that be?" the killer asked.

"I want you to kill McCoy for me."

Banks didn't hesitate. "How much?"

"I'll double what you're already getting."

Banks nodded. "Fine. I'll want the money before I leave town."

"You might need to hurry," Wade told him. "Word is they're leaving town tomorrow to go after the buffalo."

"I'll do it tonight. Now, I need a room."

"They've got plenty here," Miles said. "Meanwhile, I have other business to conduct."

* * *

"Son of a bitch!" McCoy growled loudly. "I damned well can't believe that bastard went and did it."

Creed looked up from where he was seated at the table in the Cottage. "What's wrong?"

"Miles bought Reynolds' herd."

"How?"

"The ramrod sold it to him so he could pay off the hands," McCoy told him.

"How much?" asked Creed.

"Ten dollars a head."

The Texan sucked in a sharp breath. "That's—"

"—damned robbery is what it is. But since we don't have a buyer in town, it leaves everything wide open for Miles."

"What about the Broken W herd?" Creed asked.

"Warriner is talking about moving them to Sedalia. If he does, that will be three herds I have lost out on."

"All the more reason this plan of yours has to succeed."

Creed got up from the table. McCoy asked him, "Where are you going?"

"To get some answers."

Creed left the Cottage and walked outside. He headed down the street past the Longhorn, and as he did so, he saw a mild-looking man wearing a black suit sitting on the veranda and leaning his chair back against the wall. Creed glanced at him as he walked by, and the man did the same thing before he said, "Nice seeing you, Mr. Creed."

The Texan stopped. "Do I know you?"

"Maybe not," the man allowed. "Rudy Banks, at your service."

Creed's mind ran through name after name as he tried to figure out who this man was. The name was familiar...

He drew in a sharp breath as he recalled how he had heard of Rudy Banks. A man by that name was rumored to be a killer for hire, although the authorities had never been able to prove any charges against him. Banks had made his way into the files of the Faraday Security Service, though.

"How do you know me?" Creed asked.

"You're famous," Banks said. "Saw you at the train this morning. I thought it was you, but I wasn't sure. Now I am."

"What do you mean, famous?" the Texan inquired.

"Marshal Jack Theron out of Glory, Colorado, posted a dodger on you for the kidnapping of his nephew," Banks informed him.

"He was taken in lawfully. He was wanted for murder. That poster won't stand up in a court of law."

"I guess it doesn't matter much to him whether it does or not," Banks surmised. "He posted two thousand dead or alive. Word is dead is better since Lucky was hanged a few days ago."

Creed let his hand drop to his side. "You figure

on cashing in?"

Banks smiled coldly. "No, I have other business."

The Texan thought for a moment. "You say you got off the train this morning?"

Banks shook his head. "Nope. Said I saw you there."

"What business do you have here, Banks?"

"Personal."

"Meaning?"

"Meaning it isn't any of yours."

Creed nodded. "I can abide by that."

"You'll have to. Be seeing you around, Creed."

"Maybe. We'll see."

The Texan left him sitting there and continued to make his way along the street until he found the building he was looking for. Going inside, he discovered the man he sought standing behind a large bench, working on a saddle. The man looked up, noticed Creed, and said, "I wondered when I'd see you."

"What did you find out?" Creed asked him.

The man's name was Harris. A thin *hombre* with a dark mustache, he was the man McCoy had mentioned as the closest thing Abilene had to a doctor right now.

"The victim had a small hole at the base of his skull where something was inserted and pushed up into his brain. Death would have been instant."

"What would the killer have used to do it?"

"Something like a doctor's probe, only a lot sharper. They'd have to have some idea of what they were doing, too. Anyone come to mind?"

Creed thought about a small, inoffensive-looking man sitting on the porch of the Longhorn, watching the world go by, and answered grimly, "Yes, I can think of one person."

covered the back with a small indistinct looking
man standing in the shadow of the bar, hes watching
the crowd, he said and answered grimly. Yes, I can
think of one pursuit.

Chapter 9

Hector Yates was certain his quarry was comfortably ensconced in the Ross River whorehouse somewhere. The question was, where?

As he entered the foyer, which was lit by a single red-shaded lamp, he stopped to let his eyes adjust to the dark room, finally perceiving the frilly drapes hanging from the rafters that covered a doorway leading to the rooms in the back. To his left was a waist-high counter, behind which a smiling woman stood. She was dressed only in a red corset that strained at every seam, and her expansive bosom threatened to spill over the top of the satin. When she spoke to him, her voice was husky, as though she were a heavy smoker.

"You looking for a girl, handsome?"

Yates shook his head, which elicited a frown from the woman. She brushed at a wisp of red hair that had sprung loose from her upswept hairstyle and fallen down in front of her face.

"Then why are you here?"

"I'm looking for someone," Yates said. "His name is Harbin."

The woman shook her head. "Never heard of him."

Hearing voices, two scantily clad soiled doves emerged from behind the curtain. The madam said, "Since he isn't here, how about one of these girls? I'll give you a cheap rate. Hell, take two for the price of one. Annabelle and Milly are available, as you can see."

Yates wasn't interested in one girl right now, let alone two. Business was his only reason for being in this dump, and he was determined to find his quarry before the man evaded him further. The last time Nate Harbin had given the law the slip, the wiry outlaw joined up with Harry Cross and his gang and held up the Kansas City Flyer and took a gold shipment. To find him, Yates needed to get past the curtain.

The Faraday agent nodded. "All right, I'll take that offer."

"Payment up front," the madam said.

Yates dug into his pocket and took out a couple of coins. He put them on the counter, and the woman picked them both up. The Faraday man frowned. "I thought you said it would be cheap."

"Bigger bed, and you've got two of my best girls," she replied. "I'm sure you won't complain once they're done with you."

As Yates approached the girls, they smiled. Annabelle took his arm while Milly parted the curtains until they passed through. Her closeness put him on edge. He wished he wasn't chasing a fugitive.

In contrast to the foyer, the rear of the establishment was functional but undecorated—one long hallway with doorways on each side closed off by more curtains. Cries of passion drifted out of each room as Yates walked past them.

At the end of the hallway, they entered a small room large enough to fit a double bed and nothing else. Annabelle nuzzled his neck and kissed the skin below his ear. "Why don't you take your clothes off?" she murmured.

Yates shook his head. "You two first. I want to watch you undress each other."

The two prostitutes shrugged and started their work. Yates waited until they were well and truly involved with each other before he slipped out through the curtain. He looked down the hall and saw the redheaded madam coming out of the room. She gave Yates a surprised, guilty look, and he knew which room Harbin was in.

"Look out!" she cried loudly, giving the wanted man as much warning as she could.

Yates pulled his Remington and thumbed back the hammer as he charged down the hall. He yanked the curtain aside and saw the pale shape of a naked man flailing beside the bed like a white whale beached on soft sand. The whore was also naked, and as soon as she saw Yates' weapon, she let out a piercing shriek.

"Hold it, Harbin!" Yates called. "I'm here to take you in."

"The hell you are," Harbin snarled as he whipped up the pistol he'd finally located on the floor.

But he was too slow, and Yates' weapon barked

first by a split-second. A black hole appeared in Harbin's chest and he stiffened, looking down as blood began flowing thick from it.

"You kilt me." He groaned and sagged back to the floor.

The whore's shrieks grew louder when she realized her customer was lying dead on the floor beside her bed.

"Oh, dear Lord," the madam gasped from behind the Faraday man.

Yates turned to her and said, "You'd best get your sheriff."

"We don't have one," she said harshly. "Why do you think Harbin was here? He knew there's no law in these parts."

"Then get your undertaker. Harbin'll need burying."

"He wouldn't have if you'd just left."

"Sorry, ma'am, but I had a job to do."

"Now you have one more," she said caustically.

"What's that?"

"Get the hell out of my establishment."

* * *

An hour after the shooting, four men rode into town and put their horses up at the livery stable, then walked down the street to the hotel. The foyer was dim, not helped by the dark wood paneling on the walls. As they came up to the counter, their leader said, "We want a couple of rooms."

The thin-faced clerk nodded. "Sure. You all just

need to sign the register."

The man turned the register around and was about to sign when a name caught his eye. He stared at it and read it a couple of times to make sure he had it right. He stabbed his finger at it and demanded, "This name here. Where is he?"

The clerk was surprised. "What?"

"The *hombre* who goes by the name of Yates on the damn register. Where is he?"

"I don't know, mister."

The man's eyes narrowed. "You don't know?"

"Ah, no. Not at this time, anyway. Besides, it's policy not to give out any information to...oh!"

The man had grabbed a handful of shirt and was dragging the clerk toward him, forcing him up on tip-toe as he leaned across the counter. The man then pulled the lapel of his coat aside to reveal his badge. "Where?"

"He was involved in a shooting earlier at the—"

"I didn't ask you what he's been doing," Jack Theron grated. "I asked you where he was. My patience is running mighty thin about now, sonny."

"Try the saloon. He might be there."

Jack let him go. "If he comes back, you don't tell him we're here, understood? Or you'll take his place."

The clerk gulped. "Sure. Not a word."

"You got the law in this town?"

"We do now," the man said with a weak attempt at a smile.

"What's that supposed to mean?" Jack demanded.

"Nothing, nothing. Forget I said it. We have no law at all."

"Fine by me," Jack growled. "Now, what about those rooms?"

* * *

When Yates left the saloon, it was well after dark. He'd had more than his share of alcohol, but it was always the same after he'd killed a man. He took no pleasure in it and saw it as a grim necessity of his work at times.

Outside, he stopped on the boardwalk and took a deep breath. Although not drunk, he was relaxed.

If he hadn't been, he would have seen the trouble coming.

The first indication was the hard barrel of a gun pressed firmly against his spine. The second thing was the iron-hard voice that said, "We been looking for you."

* * *

The Faraday man's body was discovered the next morning, hanging from the rafters in the stable. It was obvious that he'd been beaten badly before being strung up. With no law in the town, the hostler cut the body down and called for the undertaker, who was delighted by the increase in business over the past twenty-four hours.

The undertaker found Yates' badge and bona fides and realized there might be more money to be made than just the small amount of cash he discovered among Yates' belongings. After the burial, the man sent word to the Faraday office in Washington regarding the agent's death. Maybe somebody there would feel grateful enough for the notification to send along a little something in return.

Even if they didn't, it never hurt to have a man like Matthew Faraday in your debt, no matter how small that debt was.

The message landed on Faraday's desk three hours after it had been sent. The agency owner took one look at the message, balled up the paper, and threw it across the room.

First that cattle buyer and now Yates. At first glance, no connection existed between the two killings. However, Faraday picked up another sheet of paper that had arrived on his desk that morning. In bold letters across the top, it said, WANTED!

It was explanation enough for why Yates had been murdered the way he had been. However, there was one other man listed on the bogus poster, and it was only a matter of time before someone tried to cash in on the reward.

* * *

The same evening Hector Yates was killed, Joseph McCoy walked out of the Drover's Cottage and across the rail line to the yards, which should have been full of cattle ready to be shipped. However, they were all out on the plains, waiting for a buyer to come or, in the case of the animals Miles had bought, waiting for a train.

McCoy's dream was dying before his eyes. Even

if Creed and the others managed to round up some buffalo, there was no guarantee the plan would work. McCoy leaned against the rail and closed his eyes, listening to the distant lowing of the animals. The train would leave tomorrow, heading farther west to the buffalo's feeding grounds, where they planned to capture the animals they needed to pull off the plan McCoy had cooked up.

Creed had managed to get several cowboys to sign on for the crazy idea before they all got too drunk.

A noise floated on the cool night air, faint but audible. McCoy straightened and looked around. There was no one about that he could see. He shrugged and returned to leaning against the rail.

There was a lot riding on his idea. If he could just get the buyers back to town, more herds would come, and the money would flow. It would bring more business to Abilene, and the town would flourish. It—

The sudden pain burned deep in his back, causing the muscles to contract and his body to stiffen. He bit back a cry of pain as his teeth ground together.

The strength went out of McCoy's body, and he sank to his knees. The world started to spin, and the last thing he saw was a dark shadow looming above him.

* * *

Rudy Banks wasn't happy. He was sure the knife had hit a rib on the way in and been deflected from its course. He stood over McCoy and was bending down to finish him off when a voice called, "Joe, you out here?"

The killer muttered a curse and slipped into the shadows, leaving McCoy to lie where he'd fallen.

Creed emerged from the darkness and looked around. He would have sworn he'd seen McCoy head in this direction. He frowned and looked around for a moment more, then turned to walk across the tracks.

He heard a moan—low, almost lost in the breeze that sprang up at the same time. Creed turned back and waited. The breeze dropped, and he heard it again.

"Is there someone there?" After another moan, the Texan drew his Colt. "Joe?"

"H-here."

Creed found him where he lay. "Damn it, Joe, what happened?"

"Don't know. Pain...pain in my back."

Creed felt around and found the warm wetness. "Damn it."

He could go for help, but if whoever did this was still out there, they might come back. He fired his gun three times into the air.

"Hang on, Joe. We'll get you some help."

* * *

"How's he doing?" Creed asked Harris as he met the man at the bottom of the stairs in the Drover's Cottage.

"He's lucky he's still alive," the surgeon's-aide-

124

turned-saddle maker said. "I saw wounds like this in the war from bayonets, and in almost every case, they just died."

A few of the Broken W hands had arrived to help the Texan get McCoy back to the Cottage and upstairs into his bed, where he could be looked after.

"Is he going to make it?"

Harris shrugged. "I guess we'll see."

"Thanks, Doc," Creed said.

"You're forgetting one thing, Creed," Harris said.

"What's that?"

"I'm not a doctor."

"Close enough."

Harris sighed. "I'll come back to check on him in the morning."

"Thanks."

The man had just left when Liza came downstairs to report, "He's resting. Sally is with him."

"You look like you could use a drink," Creed said.

"I could use half the damn bottle," she replied.

He let out a bleak laugh. "I'll see what I can do."

"You just want to get me drunk to take advantage of me," Liza admonished him.

He held up both hands defensively, then gave her a wink. "I admit it. I'm guilty."

"You know what? I don't care. Just get me the drink, then you can have your way with me."

Creed grabbed a bottle from the bar and walked to the table where Liza had sat down. He sat as well and poured two drinks, pushing one across the scarred tabletop. Liza picked the glass up and studied it.

The Texan watched her. "Is there something wrong?"

"I'm starting to think that maybe I should have stayed back in Texas and never left home."

"I don't think you could have done that. You're not the stay-at-home type."

She tossed down the drink and placed the empty glass back on the table. "You're right. Fill it again."

Creed did as she asked, then stoppered the bottle. Liza asked him, "What happens now?"

Creed thought for a moment. "We do what we set out to. Just because McCoy is out of action doesn't mean we can't get it done. We'll be gone the best part of a week. By the time we're back, if he's still alive, he should be well on the mend."

"You're serious?"

"Don't have a choice. The railroad has invested far too much money in this town and this plan, so I have to see it through to the end. We've got the cowboys, a locomotive, and stock cars. All we need now are the buffalo."

"We're still leaving in the morning then?"

Creed hesitated. "Uh..."

Liza's gaze hardened. "Don't even think about it, John. I'm going, too. I've been part of this since before the beginning."

There was fire in her eyes, and Creed knew this was a fight he had no chance of no winning. "All right. But you know it's a good bet there are Indians around. Most likely Kiowa."

"I know," Liza allowed. "But I'm going anyway. If Hawk is, then I am."

Creed threw his drink back and said, "All right then. Be ready in the morning."

He got up from the seat and went upstairs, where he found Sally still with McCoy. The man was awake but weak, and it took all his strength when he tried to talk.

"Just be quiet and listen, Joe," Creed told him. "I'm taking the train out in the morning, and we'll get your buffalo for you. We'll be gone the better part of a week, I reckon."

The man looked as though he was about to protest, but Creed cut him off. "We'll be fine. You just concentrate on getting better. By the time we get back, you'll be just about ready to ride to Chicago w…you don't know…"

"Don't know what?"

"Buffalo. Hard, killers."

"I picked us some top Texas hands, Joe. We'll be fine."

"Be…be careful. Kiowas," McCoy managed to get out.

"I will, Joe. You just get better." Creed patted him on the back of the hand and left the room. He went downstairs and saw Warriner from the Broken W sitting alone at a table. The Texan walked over to him and said, "Mind if I sit?"

The trail boss looked at him and shook his head. "Be my guest."

Creed sat and stared across the table. "I need to ask a favor."

"Ask away."

"I need you to ride herd on McCoy while I'm gone.

Whoever tried to kill him is still out there, and they might well try again."

"You're still going tomorrow then?"

"Yes."

Warriner nodded. "The way I figure it is that if McCoy gets himself killed, then his plan goes up in smoke, and I'll have to sell my herd to that bastard Miles. I'll burn in Hell before I do that."

"Thanks, Bernie," Creed said. "Now, about Miles. Keep an eye on him. He and his crew are dangerous."

"I can handle them."

"There is another killer in town, and I think he's responsible for at least one death so far and possibly Joe being stabbed."

Warriner leaned forward in his seat. "Who might that be?"

"A man named Rudy Banks."

"The Man in Black?"

"You've heard him called that too, huh?" Creed asked.

"I have," Warriner said grimly. "They say he learned how to kill in the war...and learned to enjoy it. I have friends among the Rangers down in Texas. I've heard of him, all right."

Creed got up from the table. "Thanks again, Bernie."

"You want any more men?"

"No, we'll be fine."

Creed hoped his confident prediction turned out to be true.

* * *

When news on the attack on McCoy filtered back to Hank Miles at the Longhorn, he was less than impressed and sought Banks out to let him know. "I'm paying you good money to kill that man, yet you failed."

"It was a stroke of bad luck," Banks replied laconically. "I'll keep at it until the job is done."

"Well, the longer he lives, the higher the likelihood of him getting his scheme off the ground."

"He's going nowhere."

"Creed is. I got word he's still leaving tomorrow."

"He seems like a determined man," Banks allowed.

"You've talked to him?"

The killer nodded. "We discussed another issue he has."

"What issue?" Miles asked.

Banks told him about Jack Theron's quest for vengeance. "If you really want Creed gone, there's the way."

Miles rubbed his chin and frowned in thought. "You might just have something there. Let the law do my work for me."

"Just let me kill him," Wade suggested. "That'd be a hell of a lot simpler, boss."

"No," Miles said. "I have another plan for you. The Broken W herd. I need Warriner out of the way if I'm going to get my hands on it."

Wade mumbled something under his breath that Miles couldn't quite make out. "What was that?" he snapped.

"I said, for all time we've been here, we might as well stay and take over the town ourselves."

Miles stared at him for a moment before saying, "You know, Rio, I might just do that. But first, I need to wake the telegrapher up. He's going to have a busy night, trying to find Jack Theron."

Chapter 10

The sun had not long poked its nose above the horizon when the train pulled out of Abilene on its journey west. Behind the Baldwin were two stock cars and a passenger car, while bringing up the rear was a small baggage car containing most of the cowboys' equipment. Inside the passenger car, Creed sat opposite Liza and Hawk as the landscape steadily slipped by outside. The other cowboys Creed had hired played cards or talked, filling the car with the low hum of conversation.

They passed through Salina, then Ellsworth, and traveled for another three hours, passing through Hays City before the train slowed and eventually stopped.

They disembarked and set up camp in a shallow depression not far from the train to give them shelter from the wind. The horses were taken from the second stock car and tethered while the hands began building a makeshift corral in which hold the buffalo.

Creed left that up to Hawk. He saddled his mount and rode across the plains to the south with Liza by his side.

The terrain rolled until they were about four miles from the rail line, which was where they found the buffalo, great shaggy beasts that snorted and grunted as they moved around the prairie. The plain ahead of them rippled with the brown mass.

"Oh, good Lord," Liza said as they reined in. "There's thousands of them."

"You've never seen them before?" Creed asked her.

"Not like this. Nothing like this. It's amazing."

"Just keep an eye out for Indians," Creed said. "A herd this size is bound to attract them."

They gazed at the scene before them until Creed decided it was time to go back. "We'll make a start on rounding them up tomorrow. I think three will do."

"Is it going to be hard?"

"It very well might be. And it will be dangerous."

Turning away from the herd, they began making their way back along the trail they'd followed. If they'd stayed a few moments longer, they might have seen the three riders emerge from a gully to the southeast.

* * *

That evening, they sat around the campfire, talking about possible plans for the following day. An older hand who went by the name of Switch said, "I think if we split up into teams of three, we can see how that goes."

Creed nodded. "I think you might be right. They're powerful animals. It'll take more than one rope to bring them under control. Once you have one, bring it back here."

"There's another problem we're gonna face," a second lean Texan said. "The herd ain't going to just stop in one spot. It'll keep moving to look for feed."

"Then we'd better get what we need fast," Creed said.

"Might be easier said than done," Switch told them. "I saw one of them bulls run right over a horse and rider one time. Just put his head down and went right over them. Killed horse and rider both."

"Which means you don't do anything stupid," Creed said. "There are twelve of us. Three groups of three and the other three will keep watch for Indians. This is a big herd, so we need to keep an eye out."

"What do you want us to do?" Ernie the fireman asked.

"We've got a couple of spare rifles. You and Lance can watch over the camp."

He nodded. "Fair enough."

Somewhere out on the prairie, a coyote howled. It was answered by another. Creed looked around at the men and said, "Three of you take first watch. The rest turn in."

Hawk stood up. "I'll do it."

"Me, too," said Switch.

Creed nodded. "I'll join you."

He stood up, grabbing his Winchester as they began walking toward the edge of the camp. Once they were out of earshot, Switch said, "Y'all heard the same thing I did, right?"

They nodded. Creed said, "I wasn't expecting visitors on the first night."

"Let's hope they're just looking," Hawk added.

"Don't skyline yourselves, and make sure whoever comes on watch after you doesn't either."

They spread out around the camp, keeping below the rim of the depression that housed their camp. The moon was high in the sky, but it was quite cloudy, so there were few occasions when the light actually shone. At one point, Creed thought he saw movement out on the prairie, but a cloud scudded across the moon and brought darkness with it. When it cleared, whatever was there, if anything, was gone.

Creed turned in after a couple of hours and didn't rouse until Hawk shook him awake the following morning. With the dawn came bad news: they'd lost three horses and one of the nighthawks.

"Who?" snapped Creed, irritated that this could even happen.

Hawk's face grew grim. "Liza."

* * *

Creed finished buckling on his gun belt and rammed his hat onto his head with a frustrated sigh. "How the hell did this happen?"

"I don't know. Maybe she was just trying to do her bit. She rode many a nighthawk on the herd as we came up from Texas."

134

Creed shook his head. She would, independent as she was. "How long ago?" Creed asked as he picked up his saddle.

"Four, five hours."

"Do we know how many?"

"Four of them."

"Indians?"

"Only one of them was riding an unshod horse. Doesn't mean anything. Could be Kiowas out raiding, and they picked up some shod horses somewhere."

Creed retrieved his horse from the corral and threw the saddle on its back. When he'd finished with the cinch and dropped his stirrups, he put his Winchester into the scabbard and turned to Hawk. "You're in charge while I'm gone. If I'm not back in five days, I'm not coming back."

"What about Liza?"

"She'll be long gone, too," he replied as he hoisted himself into the saddle.

"Bring her back, Creed."

The Texan nodded. "I intend to."

He heeled the horse out of the depression. At the top, he stopped, then slowly rode around looking for sign until he found it. Hawk was right; there had been four of them. One horse was unshod, and there was one that had a nick in its offside fore shoe. Their tracks headed south toward Indian territory.

Creed kneed his horse forward and rode after them, following the trail for an hour before losing it among the trampled grass and churned earth left by the passing buffalo herd. The next two frustrating hours were spent trying to pick it up again. When he did, they had changed course to the southeast. The lost time put him even farther behind them, and who knew what they were doing to Liza?

* * *

Alighting from the passenger car, a well-dressed gray-haired man looked around, noting that he was the only passenger who had departed the train in Abilene.

Further along the train, a conductor walked toward him with a small bag in his hand. Matthew Faraday held out his hand to take it and the beady-eyed conductor dropped it at his feet, staring at him coldly. The man's thin mouth held a chaw of tobacco, and he spat a stream of juice into the dirt at the agency owner's feet. Some of it splashed onto his boots.

"I do wish you hadn't done that," Faraday said quietly.

The conductor squinted at him and spat once more. His defiance elicited a movement so swift it was hard to detect with the naked eye.

Faraday hit the man, catching him in the throat. The conductor's eyes bulged, and his mouth dropped open so brown juice spilled down his chin.

"Maybe next time, you might show passengers a little more respect."

Faraday leaned down and picked up his small bag, tipping his hat to the stunned man as he wished him a good day. He walked toward the end of the train before crossing the tracks, then headed to the Drover's Cottage. Behind him, the conductor stumbled around, still gasping for breath.

* * *

"You might be on the older side, but you look handsome enough," Sally said to Faraday when she laid eyes on him.

"Don't let the gray hair fool you, my dear," he replied. "If I felt any better, I'd be dangerous."

She eyed him curiously from where she stood behind the counter. "Maybe I might find that out."

He gave her a wry smile. "I'm looking for a room."

"Got plenty of them," she replied.

"I only need one."

"I'll get you a key."

She turned away. Faraday said, "Can you tell me where to find a man called John Creed?"

Her hand froze above the key before picking it up. She turned back and said, "He's not in town."

"He's gone out with McCoy?" Faraday asked.

She eyed him questioningly. "You know about that?"

"I should. I'm the man who sent Creed here."

Sally seemed to relax. "They left yesterday. All except Joe, that is."

Faraday frowned. "Oh?"

"Someone tried to kill Joe, and he's upstairs in bed."

Concern appeared on Faraday's face. "Is he going to make it?"

"The man who patched him up seems to think so."

"Take me to him."

"What about your room?" she asked.

"We can do that later."

He followed her upstairs to the room where McCoy lay recuperating. Outside the door sat a cowboy armed with a Winchester. "Who's he?" the guard asked.

"He's okay," Sally said. "He's come to see Joe."

"All right then," the cowboy said as he let the hammer down on the carbine.

They entered the dark room with drawn curtains. Sally walked over to the drapes, pulled them back, and pushed the double windows out, allowing a gust of fresh air to rush through the opening.

"You awake, Joe?" she asked.

"I wasn't," McCoy mumbled.

"Man here to see you."

"Who?"

"I'm Matthew Faraday, Mr. McCoy," he said. "I came here to see if I could help and warn my man about trouble coming his way."

"You mean, Creed?"

"Yes."

"He's out with the others getting the buffalo."

"So I heard. Anyway, why don't you fill me in on what I've missed?"

* * *

The shot came out of the night like a lead lance. It tore through the darkness and burned a furrow across the left forearm of Bernie Warriner, leaving ragged and bloody flesh.

Instead of taking cover, the cattleman cursed up a storm and pulled his gun from its holster, then started firing in the direction the shot came from. Eventually, the hammer clicked on an empty chamber, and the trail boss cursed some more.

The gunfire echoes died and he stood there reloading, unconcerned about whether whoever had taken the shot at him was still around. A crowd began to gather, with them those of his men who had stayed in Abilene. When one asked what had happened, he snarled, "Some bushwhacking son of a bitch thought he'd take a shot at me. He learned the hard way that if you don't put Bernie Warriner down first try, you don't get another chance."

"You killed him?" a newcomer asked.

"I doubt it," the trail boss growled. "But I sent enough lead his way to make him reconsider the choices he made." Warriner stared at the well-dressed newcomer. "Who are you, anyway?"

"Matthew Faraday."

"I heard of you from that fella who works for you. How'd you like a drink?"

"Sure. I'll buy."

Warriner grinned. "Mr. Faraday, I'm likin' you already."

* * *

Sally patched up Warriner's arm while they sat in the saloon, sipping whiskey. Once she was done, she left the two men to talk. The trail boss said, "What brings you to Abilene, Faraday?"

"I didn't like the reports I was receiving," Faraday replied. "Things seemed to be getting out of hand."

"You could say that. A cattle buyer was killed, and so was Reynolds from the Triangle T. Max Kelly's herd got stolen and Creed found it in Ellsworth. Except the man who stole them is friends with the governor and, well, you can guess how that went. Somebody tried to kill McCoy and now me."

"Does it get any better?" Faraday asked dryly.

"Oh, yeah. The Man in Black is in town."

"Who?"

"Rudy Banks, the assassin."

Faraday leaned forward, frowning. "What did Creed make of that?"

"He's all but certain Banks was the one who killed the buyer and tried to put McCoy in Boot Hill. That means that Banks is workin' for Hank Miles."

Faraday sighed.

"You asked," Warriner said.

Faraday nodded and said, "Yes, I suppose I did."

* * *

"What the hell happened?" Miles growled savagely at Rio Wade.

"I missed, all right?" Wade shot back at his boss. "The son of a bitch stood there like he was invincible and threw lead all over the place. He almost put a slug in my head. By the time he ran dry, there were people starting to gather around. I'll get him next time."

Miles looked across the room at Banks. "Since

you've proven that you can't kill McCoy, how about you try something a little easier?"

"I told you I'd fix it," Wade said.

"You had your chance," Miles snapped, losing his patience.

"McCoy will die soon," Banks said. "But if you want, I can take care of the trail boss, too."

"Good. Get it done."

"I saw someone get off the train today," Banks said. "Thought you might be interested."

"Who?"

"Matthew Faraday."

"You know him?"

Banks shrugged. "Never talked to him. Have seen him from afar."

"What would he be doing here?"

Another shrug. "Let's see. You killed, or rather, I killed his buyer. You killed the trail boss, Reynolds, and stole a herd. Should I go on? Everything you've done so far affects the railroad, and seeing as he runs the top security agency for it and others, naturally, what you do will draw attention."

"Then we kill him too."

Banks shook his head, a sorrowful expression on his face. Miles frowned. "What?"

"You want my honest opinion on this?" the killer asked.

"Sure."

"You keep killing people, and you're going to have federal law raining down upon you from everywhere. You're losing sight of the prize, which is stopping McCoy from making Abilene a viable railhead. Isn't that right?"

"That's right."

"What's he pinned all his hopes on?"

"The buffalo idea," Miles said.

"Right. You need to stop that from happening, not just kill everyone who upsets you."

"It solves a problem—"

"And creates another as it gets out of hand."

"So?"

"From what I've heard, he has one stop on the way to Chicago, providing that he gets his buffalo—St. Louis. That'll create one opportunity for you to do something before they reach their destination. If you fail there, then you still have Chicago."

"I still want that herd," Miles growled.

"If you stop McCoy's buffalo idea, then you'll get your herd," Banks pointed out. "Do you know people in St. Louis and Chicago who might help you?"

"I do, as a matter of fact."

"Then you might want to let them know what's possibly coming their way."

Miles nodded. "What about you?"

"Me? I'm going to sit back and watch it all happen. This could be mighty interesting."

"There is still one thing you haven't factored into this plan of yours," Miles pointed out. "Jack Theron."

Banks grinned. "Yes, sir, mighty interesting."

* * *

That night while most people slept, a lone rider left Abilene and headed east, carrying a message in his breast pocket. He was to take it to Junction City, where he would go to the telegraph office to send it out. It was marked urgent, and it was destined for St. Louis, Kansas City, Wichita, and Salina.

* * *

Ed Gaylord stood leaning on a pitchfork, watching riders approach the livery stable around mid-morning the following day. He was grateful for the break from tossing hay, but these men had a look about them that oozed trouble. The sun flashed off the star pinned to the lead rider's chest as he drew his mount to a halt in front of the livery owner.

"You got stalls for four horses?" the man growled.

"Yes, sir. Got plenty of stalls."

"Then you can put our horses in them."

"I can do that, I guess."

The riders dismounted. The leader asked, "Where might I find a fella named Miles?"

"I think he's been staying over at the Longhorn Saloon," Gaylord told him.

"Uh-huh. What about Creed?"

The hostler noticed how the lawman's eyes narrowed when he mentioned the name. "He ain't here. Left with the train the day before yesterday."

"What do you mean, left?"

"He'll be back in a few days," Gaylord added hurriedly, moving backward and placing the pitchfork between them when the lawman took a menacing step toward him.

"He'd better be. I ain't sittin' around here wasting

my time when I could be out there hunting a killer."

Gaylord raised an eyebrow. "A killer?"

"That's right. The man is a killer, and I'm here to see that he pays for it. Now, take care of the damned horses."

They left the stable and crossed the tracks, then walked into the Longhorn and trudged up to the bar. Jack Theron leaned against it and caught sight of a man in the mirror he thought he recognized. Turning, he stared at the man dressed in black seated at the table near the front window.

"Good thing I ain't here for you or I'd kill you now, you little snake," Jack growled.

"Good thing you didn't try because you'd already be dead," Banks retorted.

"What are you doing in this burg, Banks?" Jack growled.

"Get yourself a bottle, Jack, and I'll tell you."

"I've got other pressing business."

"If you're talking about Creed, he's not in town. Won't be back for a few days."

The lawman shot a glance around the room to see who might be listening to their words and saw that Banks was the only one there. "Where is everyone?"

"No buyers, no business."

The barkeep appeared from the back room, carrying a couple of bottles he'd just filled. He glanced at the four men standing at the bar and asked, "What can I do for you?"

"Give us a couple of bottles," Jack said.

The man placed the ones in his hands on the counter and the lawman scooped one of them up, along with a glass. "Pay the man, Tyrone."

Jack crossed to Banks' table and sat down. The killer took his right hand out from under the table and placed a small Smith & Wesson revolver on the tabletop. "Never can be sure of some people these days."

"You here on business, Banks?" Jack asked.

"Something like that. You, on the other hand, are on the revenge trail, I believe."

"After the bastard that got Lucky hung," Jack replied.

"It was bound to happen, Jack," Banks pointed out. "After all, he was known for getting up to mischief."

"He was family; that's all that matters."

"If you say so."

"I do."

Jack poured himself a drink. He held the glass up and said, "Here's to a quick death."

Chapter 11

The sod-built structure seemed to grow out of the ground. No one knew how long it had been there or who'd originally erected it. What was known, however, was that it was a place where travelers could call for food, water, and rest. Part trading post, part waystation without the stagecoaches, it was run by a man named Hunsicker. He'd taken it over from someone named Roberts, who'd been killed by an outlaw named Farrell. Roberts had obtained it from a German named Schmidt. Maybe he'd been the one who'd built it.

That morning, however, Hunsicker was out at the corral tending a traveler's horse when he noticed the five riders headed his way from the north. At first, he wasn't sure who they were, but that changed as they drew nearer.

"Why the hell did they have to come back here," he muttered to himself. Then he saw they had a woman with them, along with some extra horses. "That can't be good."

The riders were led by a man named Cox. He was a wide-framed killer with a small scar on his cheek. He'd been a Kansas raider during the war before branching out on his own. Now he made a living by any means possible.

With him rode a young killer named Junior Merrett, a lanky kid who thought taking human life was nothing more than sport. Then there was Tucker, an old plainsman who found it easier to get what he required by killing for it. Lastly came the Kiowa, Blood Elk. He'd stumbled into their camp one night, half-dead with a bullet in his back. For some reason, Cox had removed the bullet instead of letting him die. The others still couldn't work out why, but the Kiowa had remained with the group after he was better. He was the one who led the horses they'd stolen.

Liza trailed behind Cox on a tired bay. Her hands were tied behind her back, and her thighs ached from having to grip the swaying mount to stay atop it.

They eased to a stop outside the soddy where Hunsicker stood. Cox looked at him and said, "Got some horses to sell if you're interested."

Hunsicker wanted to say no, but Cox was a man to be afraid of. "I might be."

"There's three of them. I want a hundred each," Cox stated.

Hunsicker shook his head. "I can't afford that. Twenty."

Cox glared at the man. "You insulting me, Hunsicker?"

"No."

"Then you better come up with some more money."

He looked at the woman for the first time. She was scared and tired. He said, "I'll give you a hundred for each horse if you throw the woman in for another fifty."

He didn't want the woman, but she'd be better off with him than with Cox.

Cox chuckled. "You're a damned thief, Hunsicker. If you think I'm putting the woman into the deal, you're a mite more touched in the head than I figured. A hundred each without the woman."

"I'll give you fifty each and throw in two bottles of buffalo piss."

Cox nodded. "Deal."

"What about the woman?"

"I already told you, you can't have her. I'm taking her south, where I'll get more for her than what you can offer me. You got somewhere I can keep her?"

"Got an underground root cellar."

"That'll do."

"How long are you staying?" Hunsicker asked.

"Long enough," Cox told him.

"Long enough for what?"

"Long enough to kill the man who's trailing us." Hunsicker pulled a face. "Now, hold on!"

"Don't get all uppity, Hunsicker. We'll kill him and be on our way."

"Who is the fella who's after you, anyway?"

"I don't know." Cox nodded at the prairie. "Why don't you go out and ask him?"

Hunsicker turned to look at the plains and saw the solitary rider sitting astride his horse, not moving and outside of rifle range. "That's him?"

"As far as we can tell."

"Just let me go out there and kill him," Merrett said confidently. "You know I can."

"Just see to the horses," Cox said flatly. "I'm hungry. You got something to eat, Hunsicker?"

The man swallowed hard, not taking his eyes off the rider. "I'll find something."

* * *

Creed sat there on his horse while the men did what they needed to. He was sure they had put Liza in a root cellar of some kind and gone inside. After catching up to them the day before, he'd been dogging them. The territory had flattened out some, and getting close enough to them to do something was next to impossible. But he was certain, judging by the air sweeping off the plains, there would be a storm that evening, and that would be his chance to get Liza back.

In the meantime, he just sat and watched.

* * *

"Where do you think you're going?" Cox asked Hunsicker.

"I'm going to take this food to the woman," he replied.

The outlaw stared at him for a moment before

nodding. "All right. Just don't be gone too long."

Hunsicker opened the door and stopped where he was. "He's still there, you know?"

Cox rose to his feet and walked over to the door. He looked out across the prairie and saw the rider, still there atop his horse.

"Persistent son of a bitch, ain't he?"

"Maybe you should just let the woman go and he'll leave," Hunsicker said.

"Maybe you should just shut the hell up and take the food to her."

With a nod, Hunsicker walked outside and turned toward the root cellar. He hurried over to it and opened the door before going inside. He found Liza tied up and seated on the damp earthen floor.

"I brought you some food, miss," he said quietly.

"You know what you can do with your food," Liza shot back at him.

"You have to eat. Keep your strength up."

"Go to hell," she spat.

"Your friend is still out there."

That got her attention.

"He's been out there all this time, and it don't look like he's going anywhere soon," Hunsicker told her. "Who is he?"

"If I'm right, he's the man who's going to kill every last one of you."

"Miss, I'm not with Cox and the others. In fact, I tried to buy you to get you away from him," Hunsicker explained.

"That makes you just as bad," Liza snorted.

"No, ma'am. I told him he should let you go, but

he won't."

"Then you let me go," she said, a hint of desperation in her voice.

"I can't. He'll kill me."

"You're all talk."

"Have they hurt you any?" he asked, untying her hands so she could eat.

"Not yet."

Hunsicker nodded at the plate of food he put on the floor beside her. "Eat. I'll stand over near the door and wait until you've finished."

Liza ate the food and handed the plate back to Hunsicker, who said, "I'll get you some water shortly."

"Thank you."

"Keep the faith, miss," he said. "I have a feeling it'll all work out for you."

"Do you now?"

Hunsicker spun around to see Merrett standing in the doorway. "You plan on doing something stupid, Hunsicker?"

"I won't have to," he replied. "I think that fella out there will do it all himself."

"If he was going to do something, he would have done it by now." The young killer sneered.

"If you say so."

"What are you saying, Hunsicker?"

"Nothing. It's just that whoever it is out there on the plains has you four mighty spooked."

"Are you saying I'm scared?" Merrett asked. His eyes blazed, and his jaw set firmly as his anger rose. "Because I ain't scared of no one."

"Sure, kid."

Those two words were enough to push the killer over the edge. "I'll show you," he snarled and whirled away.

Hunsicker followed him outside, closely shadowed by Liza. They watched as he stormed over to the corral and grabbed a saddle off the top rail.

"What have you done?" Liza asked.

"Hopefully made it easier for your friend."

The horses milled as Merrett tried to get the saddle on one, eventually succeeding. He got the cinch tightened and led the horse out of the corral. Cox appeared in the doorway of the sod hut.

"Where are you going, kid?"

"I ain't a coward, Cox," Merrett shouted.

"Never said you were, but that don't answer my question."

Merrett swung into the saddle and spun the horse so it pointed at the prairie. He drew his gun and shouted once more, "I ain't a damned coward!"

He gave the horse a savage kick, and the animal leaped forward. Before it had gone ten yards, it was running hard.

Tucker and Blood Elk came outside to see what the commotion was about. Tucker asked, "What's put the burr under his saddle?"

"How the hell should I know?" Cox snapped.

They all stood in silence as the young killer rode hard in the direction of the lone figure on the prairie atop his horse, not moving.

* * *

Creed sat easy in his saddle, watching the rider come toward him. Whatever he was up to couldn't be good. Thunder rumbled in the western sky as steel-gray clouds started to back up on the horizon. Suddenly a sharper crack joined it, then the bullet whined past, missing by quite a bit but close enough to hear.

The horse beneath Creed shifted nervously for a moment before the Texan patted it calmingly on its muscular neck. Then he took the Winchester from the scabbard and levered a round into the chamber.

The rider coming toward him fired again, and this time the bullet passed closer than the last. Creed sighted along the barrel of the Yellow Boy and let out a slow breath. He squeezed the trigger, and the weapon slammed back against his shoulder.

The rider coming toward him suddenly threw his arms up and disappeared over the horse's rump. He crashed sickeningly to the ground, arms and legs flopping like a child's rag doll.

Creed worked the lever once more and then laid the rifle across his thighs. He didn't have to worry. The man would never get back up. Beneath him, his horse settled once more as the riderless horse galloped past them. Then he went back to watching and waiting.

* * *

"Stupid young hothead," Cox muttered. He glanced at Hunsicker. "What was all that about?"

The man shrugged.

Cox eyed him suspiciously. "Get her back in the

root cellar. And make sure she's tied up good. We're leaving tomorrow."

Hunsicker turned to the woman. "I have to."

She nodded and went back into the root cellar. Once inside, she said, "Thank you."

"What for?"

"For helping."

"Ma'am, I ain't done nothing yet. It's all up to that stranger out there. Who is he, anyway? Do you know him?"

"I know him," Liza said. "It has to be him."

"Who?"

"You'll meet him soon enough."

* * *

"He's gone," Tucker said with more than a hint of urgency.

"What do you mean, he's gone?" Cox asked as he climbed out of his chair.

A clap of thunder rocked the sod hut as lightning lit the sky and the torrential rain that fell in sheets. Cox saw, when he looked out the window after another bright flash, that the plain was empty. "He's right."

The Kiowa joined them at the window. He waited for the lightning, then grunted before walking toward the door.

"Where are you going?" Cox growled.

"Get woman."

Cox nodded. "Be careful."

The only reply was another grunt as he opened

the door, letting in a harsh gust of wind carrying moisture from the darkness. He seemed not to worry about it as he walked outside and slammed it behind him.

"You figure he'll be all right?" Tucker asked his boss.

"He's a damned Kiowa. He'll be fine."

* * *

The door to the root cellar creaked open, and Liza straightened with a start. She waited for it to swing wide, and when it did, lightning flashed and illuminated the figure in the doorway.

"Liza?"

It was Creed.

"I'm here," she said quietly, trying to control her excitement.

Creed said, "Stay here. I'll be back. I just wanted to make sure you were all right."

"Where are you going?" she asked.

"To finish it."

He disappeared and closed the door. Liza was left alone in the dark once more.

The night was pierced by a loud shriek, followed by the cracks of gunshots. Liza stiffened and waited for an indication that Creed was okay, but there was no such thing. Just another flash of lightning and the boom of thunder.

* * *

"That was him, I know it," Tucker stated for the third time. "I'd know that screech anywhere."

"What do you want me to do about it?" Cox snarled.

"One of us should go check."

"By one of us, you mean me?" Cox queried.

"I didn't say that."

"You didn't have to," Cox said knowingly. "We're staying right here. Bar the door."

"What about the woman?"

"He can have her."

"You think that's all he's going to want?"

Cox said nothing. He thought for a moment, then said, "Hunsicker, come here."

"What is it?"

"Go out there and find him. Tell him he can have the girl."

"You want me to go? What makes you think he won't shoot me?"

"What makes you think I won't if you don't?"

Right then, Hunsicker knew his chances were better out there than inside with the outlaws. He walked toward the door, putting on his hat before going out into the storm.

* * *

Hunsicker had no idea where he was going or where he would find the man. The root cellar seemed like the best place to start. Lightning flashed and the blue light reflected off the groundwater, illuminating the large bump between him and his destination. He walked forward. More lightning streaked across the sky, quickly followed by a loud boom. He jumped, couldn't help it, then took a couple more steps and reached whatever lay in front of him.

He peered down, trying to see in the dark. Another bolt of lightning flashed, and he recoiled in horror at what the light revealed. Lying in the muck on the ground at his feet was the Kiowa, eyes wide, mouth open, and a hole in his forehead.

"Give me a reason why I shouldn't kill you right now," a harsh voice growled in Hunsicker's ear.

"I'm not with them," Hunsicker said hurriedly.

"The root cellar. Move."

Creed pushed him along in front of him. They reached the door, and Hunsicker opened it. The Texan shoved him inside, and he stumbled before regaining his feet.

"Creed?" Liza said. "Are you okay?"

"Yeah."

"It's so damned dark in here," she said.

"There's a lantern and matches," Hunsicker offered.

"Find them," Creed snapped.

The man stumbled around in the dark until he found what he wanted behind a crate of supplies. He lit a match, and it flickered to life. He put it to the wick of the lantern.

Once the cellar had light, Creed said, "Why were you outside? Looking for me?"

Hunsicker nodded. "Yes, but not for what you think."

"He's all right, John," Liza said. "He's not like them."

"Prove it."

"Cox told me to come out here and tell you to take the woman and go," Hunsicker said.

The Texan shook his head. "Not going to happen. This ends here."

"What are you going to do?" Liza asked.

"Give me your coat and hat," he said to Hunsicker.

"They're wet," he replied.

Creed holstered his gun and started to shrug out of his waterlogged coat. "You don't say."

* * *

"Where do you figure he's got to?" Tucker asked Cox.

"Probably run off somewhere," the outlaw replied.

"I didn't hear no shooting, so he's probably still alive."

"Maybe."

"Let's get out of here," Tucker proposed.

"And go where? We'd have to go on foot. There's no way we'd get our horses saddled."

"Well, what if—"

"What if you just shut the hell up?" Cox snarled. "You're getting on my nerves."

Tucker glared at his boss but remained silent.

Thunder crashed outside, hot on the heels of a forked lightning bolt, and the boom caused the ground to vibrate beneath their boots. It was so unexpected that both outlaws jumped. Then, just as they started to relax, the front door opened and a figure entered, hunched against the rain. The dim interior light made it hard to see the man's face, but they assumed it was Hunsicker.

"Where the hell have you been?" Cox growled.

The figure straightened, and the coat opened to reveal a fist full of Colt. Cox realized too late that it wasn't Hunsicker. With a loud curse, he tried for his gun.

The Colt in Creed's fist roared, and the slug hit the outlaw in the chest. It knocked the man back and he tried desperately to keep his feet beneath him but failed, crashing butt-first to the earthen floor.

Creed shifted his aim, cocking the hammer as he did so. The Colt stopped in line with Tucker, who was drawing his own weapon, as well as holding his left hand out in front of him as though it would stop what was about to happen.

The Colt in Creed's hand blasted once more, taking two fingers off the outspread left hand before punching into Tucker's heart and killing him instantly.

The Texan turned back to Cox, who remained sitting upright although the shock of the bullet's impact had rendered him useless. He looked up at his killer and stammered, "Who...who are you?"

"John Creed."

The left side of Cox's mouth turned up and he grunted. "Huh. The feller Jack Theron put a bounty on."

"Apparently."

"Huh."

The killer toppled onto his side and died with his eyes open.

Creed turned away and walked toward the door.

He went back out into the rain and over to the root cellar and entered the dim room. Before he had a chance to shake the water off the coat he was wearing, Liza was in his arms.

"Is it over?" she asked.

"Yes," he replied. "It's over."

Chapter 12

Linc Peters was a big man. Broad of shoulder, dark of hair, with walnut-colored skin, he walked with an air of confidence. The man's ruggedly handsome face was currently a mask of concern, however. Never had he been summoned with such urgency by his boss, especially in the middle of an assignment for the Faraday Security Service. His orders were to finish up what he was doing and get to Abilene as soon as possible.

"I just hope Roy Harris sees things my way," he grumbled sardonically.

Linc placed the telegram in his pocket and adjusted his gunbelt, then headed back to the hotel where he had a room and went upstairs. On his bed was a cutdown shotgun. He loaded it and put more cartridges into the pocket of the black coat he wore.

His boots thudded on the stairs as he descended and went back outside, where he stopped on the boardwalk and stared at the log structure across the street. Above its door was a crude hand-painted sign that read Log House.

In there were Roy Harris and two other men wanted for the derailment of a pay train outside of Omaha, Nebraska. Linc had been on their trail for the last month, and word had come from Washington that they were here in Salina. It had taken the Faraday man three days to get here and make sure they were the men he wanted.

The fact was, he still wasn't certain. The man he thought was Harris fit the description, but before he went and braced him, he wanted to be sure. Now it was too late, and he'd have to do it anyway.

Linc trudged across the muddy street, wet from the storm that had passed through the night before. The shotgun was cradled in his arms. A rider reined in his horse when he saw the Faraday man cross the street in front of him with a look of grim determination on his face.

Linc pushed through the door of the Log House, stopping just inside to quickly scan the room. A sudden hush descended over the room as every head turned to look at him, giving him the perfect opportunity to see their faces.

He spotted them seated by the small window, and the Faraday man headed in their direction. Realizing he was walking toward them, the men put their heads together, their expressions puzzled as they whispered amongst themselves.

"Roy Harris," Linc said clearly. "I'm here to take you in."

There was a sudden scramble as customers

hurried to get out of the way. Harris's eyes widened, and his hand went for his gun.

In the confined space of the barroom, the shotgun boomed like a cannon, the noise bouncing off the thick walls. Flung backward by the blast, Harris hit the wall, along with the chair he had been sitting on. The wooden seat gave way, and the dead outlaw crumpled to the floor.

With one barrel remaining, Linc shifted his aim and squeezed the trigger again. This time one of Harris's two sidekicks went down, arms and legs flailing.

The Faraday man dropped the scattergun and pulled his Colt. As it cleared leather, he thumbed back the hammer. The remaining man had managed to get to his feet, and his gun was clear of the holster. He snapped off a panicked shot that flew a couple of feet wide of its intended target.

Linc's shot, however, didn't miss, and the bullet hammered into the man's middle. He lurched and Linc shot him again. This time he went down and stayed there.

Linc muttered a curse. He hated rushing jobs. It always ended messily, as this one had. He picked up his shotgun and turned to walk out the door. From behind the bar, the barkeep asked in a timid voice, "What...what about them on the floor that you shot?"

Linc paused in the open door and shrugged. "You'd best bury them. My work here is done."

* * *

Twenty-five-year-old Chad Rydell patted the hand of the young woman opposite him as they had morning tea together. He was a handsome man who wore a black suit and a bowler hat. His hair matched his clothes, and his shoulders stretched the fabric of his coat as he leaned forward, his smile showing even white teeth.

"Celia, darling, I need to leave St. Louis on today's train. I'm sorry."

Celia Donald pouted, her pale face sad. "But Chad, you've only just returned from Washington."

"I'm sorry, my love. I must go where Mr. Faraday wants me to."

"That man asks way too much of you," she said. "Oh, well, if you must go, then go you must. I don't know what I'll do while you're gone. How long will it be?"

"I'm not sure."

"You know Barney asked me to marry him while you were gone last time?"

The name put Rydell on edge. Barney Gibbs was one of three hoodlums in St. Louis who controlled most of the crime in the city. He, along with Frank Olsen and Lionel O'Halloran the Irishman, had sliced St. Louis into thirds. Each man stuck to their own part of the city and kept out of the others' way by gentleman's agreement.

"You need to stay away from him, Celia," Rydell said to her firmly. "That man is bad news."

"Only because he wants to marry me," Celia said haughtily.

Rydell withdrew his hand. "He's fifteen years

older than you, damn it."

"Don't you speak to me like that, Chad," Celia chided him. "I'll walk out of the café if you do."

"What do your mother and father say about him?"

Her nose lifted a little as she said, "They think he's a fine, upstanding businessman."

"They would."

"What's that supposed to mean?"

He shook his head. "Nothing. Listen, I didn't come here to fight. I wanted to spend a little time with you before I left on the train."

Celia's face softened. "We're not doing a very good job, are we?"

Rydell gave her a weak smile. "Not by half."

The door to the café opened, and two suit-wearing men entered. One was a big man with a narrow face, and the other was shorter and squarer of shoulder with a pencil-thin mustache. Rydell muttered a curse.

"What is it?" Celia asked.

He shook his head.

Celia turned hers and glanced over her shoulder and saw Barney Gibbs and Craig, his right-hand man, enter. Her head whipped back around, and she said hurriedly, "Just you watch your words. I won't have you insulting Barney with your wild accusations."

It was then that Rydell realized Celia Donald was a lost cause. Any thoughts of a future romance and maybe marriage had just been a whim. He took his napkin out of his lap and put it on the table, then reached under his coat and took his 1862

Pocket Navy Revolver from its under-arm holster. He placed it on his lap, leaving his hand on it and cocking the hammer.

"The lovely Celia Donald! What a pleasure to see you on such a fine morning," Gibbs greeted her.

She held out her hand for him to take. "You, too, Barney. Chad and I were just having morning tea before he leaves on the train today."

Gibbs' eyes grew flinty. "Really? Such a shame."

"I'm starting to think not," Rydell replied, his gaze switching to Celia and back to Gibbs.

"Oh?"

"The crime in this city is getting under my skin. Can't even have a quiet bite to eat without it coming up on you."

Celia's eyes widened. "Chad!"

The insult was out there now, and there was no going back, not that Rydell wanted to. He'd killed men like Gibbs before. That was what he did for Faraday in Washington, New York, Chicago, or any other of the larger cities where the railroad ran. There was an abundance of crime as well as gangs, and Rydell was an expert in his field.

Craig's hand moved beneath his coat, reaching for his personal weapon. Rydell's face turned to stone, and when he spoke again, his voice had a hard edge to it. "You pull that thing, and I'm going to shoot your boss, big man. Then I'm going to kill you."

Craig froze, uncertainty evident upon his face. Across the table, Celia gasped, "Chad Rydell, what are you doing?"

He ignored her.

Craig watched Gibbs, waiting for an indication of what he should do next. The hoodlum said, "It might be best if you leave St. Louis."

Rydell nodded. "Yes. I hope you two are happy together."

He got up from the table, his revolver visible in his hand. Celia asked, "Chad, what are you doing?"

"I'm leaving. Have a nice life, Celia."

"If you leave now, Chad Rydell, don't bother coming back," she called after him, throwing down the gauntlet.

He waved without turning. "That's the idea. *Adios.*"

Rydell stopped outside the café and holstered his gun. He had a train to catch.

* * *

The third man to receive a telegram instructing him to head for Abilene was Harley Moffat. Thin and in his late thirties, Moffat carried a Sharps carbine and rode a chestnut horse. Two revolvers nestled in old, well broken-in holsters attached to the gunbelt strapped around his hips. His flat-brimmed hat covered shoulder-length dark hair, and his face was unshaven.

Attired only in long johns at the time the message arrived, he had been sleeping off a two-day drunk. His arm was draped over the red-headed soiled dove beside him and he snored loudly, the sound resembling that of a pig rooting in mud.

An insistent hammering on the door woke

him. At first, he thought he was dreaming, but as it continued, the screech from beside him sounded like the cry of a mountain lion. *"Go away!"*

"What's all the noise?" Moffat groaned as he rolled onto his back.

"Some lunatic is trying to break down the door."

"Well, answer it, Dolores," Moffat said when the banging continued.

"Answer the damned thing yourself."

"Dolores, I know you're in there," a man's voice said from the other side of the door. "I can hear you."

"Damn it." She sighed.

"Who is it?" Moffat asked her.

"Robbins, the telegrapher here in Wichita."

"You going to let him in?"

"No."

"Might be important. Open the damned door before he busts the thing down."

With a muffled curse, Dolores climbed out of bed as naked as the day she was born. She turned the key and wrenched the door open. Astounded by the sight of her, Robbins' jaw about hit the floor.

"You keep staring at me like that and it'll cost you a dollar," Dolores told him.

"I...I have a telegram for Harley Moffat," the telegrapher said. He held up the slip of paper, and Dolores snatched it out of his hand. Then she casually shut the door in his face.

"What does it say?" Moffat asked from his prone position tangled in the stained sheets.

Dolores climbed onto the bed. "It says that you're to get to Abilene at your best speed."

"Who's it from?"

"Matthew Faraday."

"Damn it. I have to go."

"Who is he?"

"My boss."

"How does he know you're here?"

Moffat rolled his eyes and said, "That son of a bitch knows everything."

* * *

The fourth and last man summoned to Abilene, Briar French, was a rake-thin *hombre* who wore a suit with a top hat and carried his primary weapon under his coat in a shoulder holster, with two thin-bladed Arkansas Toothpicks also on his person. One was inside his right boot, and a split had been cut in the pants leg for easy access. The other was in a sheath fixed horizontally to his belt behind his back. His saddle gun was a Henry rifle.

French was a middle-aged man who had fought in the war like most of the men Faraday hired. The major difference was that instead of serving on the front lines like most of the soldiers, French had been a Union spy. After the war, he'd returned to life in Washington, where he'd met Matthew Faraday. One thing had led to another and French was offered a job, beginning his career as a Faraday agent.

Currently between assignments, he was in Kansas City playing poker—losing, to be precise— and he had finally worked out why. A professional gambler named Olsen was receiving hand signals from a scantily clad woman named Candy. At first, Briar had thought he was seeing things, but after the second and third times, he was certain of it. Someone should have covered the mirror before they set about cheating.

"Miss Candy," Briar said after he lost another hand.

"Yes, sugar?" she said in an atrocious imitation of a Southern accent.

"If you can't keep those fingers of yours still, I'm going to have to cut them off."

The shock on her face was instant. "Whatever do you mean, sugar?"

"I mean, the way you've been signaling this slippery gent across the table from me and letting him know what cards I have."

Two other men at the table slid their chairs back, the wooden legs scraping on the floor. The third man, Olsen, casually laid the deck of cards he was lovingly fingering on the tabletop in front of him and said, "Are you calling me a cheat, French?"

"I think 'cheat' might be a harsh word, Olsen. Nasty word, in fact. But in this case, I might be apt to use it."

"Son of a bitch," Olsen snarled.

He moved for a hideout gun, but sleight of hand didn't work for him this time. He found himself staring down the barrel of French's weapon. "Now, the question remains, am I going to kill you? The answer is, maybe. I should, but I haven't decided."

"Don't," the cheat said weakly.

"What?"

170

"Please don't."

"Maybe if you admit you were cheating."

Olsen swallowed hard, aware that everyone in the Jack High Saloon was watching. He nodded. "I was cheating, all right?"

French climbed to his feet. He took what money he thought to be his from the table and said to Olsen, "Empty your pockets."

The gambler did as he was told. Before long, all the money, including his billfold, was in the center of the table. French said, "You men take what's there."

"You can't do that," Olsen howled. "It's all I have."

"You would have taken all we have before you stopped," French pointed out. "Call it a lesson in being honest."

The other two men split the money, leaving French's part on the table, and left. French put the money in his coat pocket and said, "I'm going to walk out of here now. If you get any kind of notion to try to shoot me in the back, I wouldn't advise it because I'll kill you."

With that, French turned and walked out of the saloon.

* * *

"Mr. French?"

The Faraday agent turned to face the man who'd called after him, who was running along the boardwalk waving a piece of paper above his head. Stopping to catch his breath, the man held it out. "A message for you, sir. Came in about ten minutes ago."

French dipped his hand into his pocket and handed over a dollar before taking it. "Thank you." He read the message and nodded. "Seems we've been summoned."

He wasn't talking to the man who had delivered the telegram.

He was talking to his weapons.

Chapter 13

Creed had been gone for almost five days when he and Liza rejoined the others near the buffalo herd's grazing ground. At first, when Jack Hawk saw them, he thought they were just a couple of drifters heading north, but when they drew closer, he recognized them and felt a huge wave of relief wash over him. As they drew rein, he said, "I was beginning to think you two were dead."

"They tried," Creed told him.

Hawk looked at Liza. "You all right?"

"I'm fine."

"They didn't..."

She shook her head. "No."

He nodded. "Thank the Lord."

Creed climbed down and looked around. "How is everything going here?"

Hawk snorted. "Did you know buffalo are the orneriest, most stubborn sons of bitches to be found on God's green earth?"

"What happened?"

"We were able to corral a few of them, but when we started trying to load them yesterday, do you think they would get onto the damn car? Not on your life. They just dug them hoofs in and would not budge."

"How'd you fix it?"

"We haven't yet. I sent the train back to the nearest town for a block and tackle to drag the bastards on board."

"How many you got?"

"Four."

"It's taken you almost five days to get four buffalo?" Creed asked, surprised by the delay.

"That's right. Don't go judging us, Creed. You weren't here, so you don't have any idea what these damn critters have put us through."

After a tense couple of seconds, Creed laughed and nodded. "You're right about that. Let's go and have a look."

They went over to the makeshift corral where the buffalo were being kept. There were four large but young bulls inside, milling around. A wiry-looking cowboy sat on the top rail watching them. He glanced at Creed and Liza. "You're back."

"So it would seem," Creed replied. "How are they doing?"

"The truth? It's only a matter of time before that big cuss over there figures he can walk through this thing, and we won't have a hope in hell of trying to stop him."

Creed looked at the buffalo the cowboy indicated. He was circling the enclosure, snorting as he went.

The bull had to weigh at least two thousand pounds. They wanted bulls, sure, but not monsters. "Let him go," Creed said. "He's too big. The other three will have to do."

"You sure?" Hawk asked.

The Texan nodded. "He's over two thousand pounds of untamable beast. At least the others are around five hundred pounds lighter. They'll still be a handful. I'm surprised you even got him in here."

Hawk nodded. "All right, Skinny, let him out."

They left the cowboys to release the animal and walked toward their camp. Liza said, "I could sleep for a week."

Creed rubbed her shoulder. "Get some rest. Who knows when the train will get back."

* * *

Harley Moffat walked his mount across the tracks toward the livery stable. He found Ed Gaylord forking hay into one of the large stalls. The hostler looked up and smiled. "Welcome, stranger. Need a place for your horse?"

Moffat grunted. "Why else would I be here?"

"You're right. It's generally what people come here for."

"You got one?"

"Sure."

"I'll need a receipt?"

"A what?"

"A receipt."

"What's that?" Gaylord asked.

"It's a piece of paper that says I paid you for stabling my horse here," Moffat explained irritably.

"Never heard of it."

"You have now, and I want one, or my boss won't compensate me for it."

"Won't what?"

"You got horse apples in your ears or something?"

"Not the last time I looked," Gaylord said. "Why does your boss want the whatever-it-was again?"

"If I don't get a receipt, Faraday won't give me back the money I pay out."

"Your boss is Matthew Faraday?"

"Yes."

"Fine. Now, what was it you wanted?"

Moffat tried to resist the urge to pull one of his Army Colts from their holsters and shoot the man in the chest. It was an argument he might have lost had not Kent and Slim ventured into the livery.

"Phew, got a real stink in here," the nine-fingered outlaw said as he made an exaggerated face.

Moffat turned to face the newcomers. "You two got something you want to get off your chest?"

Slim gave him an innocent look. "No, no. What about you, Kent?"

"No, sirree."

Moffat turned back to Gaylord. He opened his mouth to speak, but Slim interrupted him. "I couldn't help but overhear the name Faraday mentioned."

"Mister," Moffat said in a low voice, "you are starting to bother me to no end. Now, I'd like to tell you this one time, and after you hear what I have to say, then you can make your own decision. I'm here on business. You seem mighty keen to push me for some reason. However, I'll only be pushed so far. Now, if you wish to continue this little soirée, I'll be more than accommodating. But I'm thinking since you have a bandage on your right hand, you can't shoot much with your left."

"I've been practicing," Slim said in a cold voice. Ever since losing his finger to Creed, anger had simmered below the surface, waiting to be released. This saddle bum would make a good target for it, to his way of thinking.

Moffat turned slowly. "You sure you want to ride this trail?"

"Yeah."

"What about you?" he asked Kent. "You dealing yourself in?"

"Maybe."

A large shadow filled the doorway behind them, a long one that made its way across the straw-covered floor to the feet of a big man who carried a cut-down shotgun.

"Damn it, Harley. You always got to find trouble wherever you go?"

"Ain't my doing this time, Linc. These gents came looking for it."

"I always told you, the way you dress attracts maggots like a week-old carcass."

"Nothing wrong with the way I dress."

"Did you just call us maggots?" Slim growled.

Linc pointed the shotgun in his direction. "You and your friend take a walk, or I'll cut you in half with this scattergun."

Knowing there was no other choice, Slim nodded at Kent. The two men backed up slowly before leaving the livery.

Gaylord chuckled. "Don't tell me, you work for Faraday too?"

"You could say that. Come on, Harley. I'll buy you a drink."

"I still have to see to my horse."

"Don't worry," the hostler said. "I'll take care of him."

Moffat nodded and grabbed his Sharps and saddlebags. He and Linc crossed the tracks and walked over to the Drover's Cottage.

"They got ladies in this place, Linc?" Moffat asked.

"Some."

Once inside, they walked over to a group of men gathered around a table near the bar. Seated were three men Moffat knew: Briar French, Chad Rydell, and lastly, Matthew Faraday.

"Howdy, Matt."

Faraday nodded. "Harley. Good to see you. Linc said he thought he saw you ride in."

"How could he see me from in here?"

"I was coming back along the street," Linc said. "You want a drink?"

"I'll have a bottle," Moffat replied.

"No, you won't," Faraday said. "You're here to work, not drink and whore. Have a glass."

Moffat scowled at his boss. "I'll have a bottle, Linc."

"Harley—"

"Damn it, Matt. Have you ever known me not to

178

get anything done because of alcohol?"

"Don't make this one the first time, Harley. This is too important."

Moffat's eyes narrowed. "What's going on?"

"There are some men in town who are here after Creed," Faraday told him. "They've already killed Hector Yates."

"Why are they still walking around then?" Moffat scowled.

"Because I'm not completely sure. That's why you are all here. Actually, your job is twofold. You're here to watch Creed's back and to ride escort on a train to Chicago."

"I knew Creed would be mixed up in this somehow," Rydell said. "He's always up to his neck in some sort of trouble."

"Gets the job done, though," Linc stated.

"He does," Faraday agreed.

"How'd he get in so deep this time anyhow?" Moffat asked.

"Lucky Theron."

"Lucky Theron?" asked French. "The Lucky Theron of the Theron Family who runs Glory over in Colorado?"

Faraday nodded. "That's him."

"He rode into their town and took him out of there?" Linc asked.

"He did. He had some help from Yates, but initially, he went in there on his lonesome."

Moffat tossed back a shot. "I like him, that nervy son of a bitch."

"It was stupid," Faraday said. "If Yates hadn't ridden

in when he did, Creed would have ended up dead."

"What happened to Lucky Theron?" Rydell asked.

"He had a date with the hangman, and Jack Theron put a bounty on Creed's head. Two thousand dead or alive. There was one on Yates, too, but they got to him first. Supposedly."

"Let's go and clean them up, then," Moffat said.

"No."

"Why the hell not?"

"Because I want to wait. I want to see if their being here has anything to do with what Creed was doing here in the first place."

"Why are we going to Chicago, boss?" Linc asked.

"We're escorting a shipment on a train."

"What kind? Gold, money?

"Buffalo."

Moffat tossed back another drink. "For a second there, I thought you said buffalo."

"I did."

"Now I know you're *loco*!"

Faraday went on to lay out the plan. After he was done, the looks on the four men's faces had not changed; they continued to look at him as though he were as crazy as when he first told them about it.

Finally, Faraday said, "There's one more thing you ought to know."

"What's that?"

"Rudy Banks is in town."

"Where?" Moffat asked, tensing.

Faraday glanced at him. "You stay away from him, Harley."

"Just as soon as I kill the son of a bitch."

"I didn't bring you here—"

"You damn well knew we had history before you even sent word for us to come, Matt. Yet here I am. Where is he?"

"Harley—"

"Where?"

"He's at the Longhorn."

Moffat climbed to his feet and started to walk out of the saloon. Faraday looked at the three remaining men, who hadn't moved. He said, "What the hell are you waiting for? Go and watch his back."

"You knew this was coming, Matthew," Linc said.

Faraday looked him in the eyes. "Maybe."

Linc climbed to his feet. "Come on. Let's go make sure he don't get backshot."

* * *

Moffat stood in the middle of the barroom like a sturdy oak in a howling thunderstorm, the Sharps in his left hand and his right hand near the Colt on his left hip. Banks sat on a chair near the far wall, a polished-top table the only barrier between him and the irate man whose intention it was to kill him. Behind Moffat, Linc ran a cautious eye over the room. He'd already picked out Jack Theron and those with him. There was another small group of men who were looking on with morbid fascination. Linc spoke out of the corner of his mouth, "You know any of them on the left?"

Briar French stared at the men and said, "I think I know one of them. Rio Wade."

"Keep an eye on them, Briar."

"With pleasure."

"Rydell, you keep an eye on our other friends."

"What about you?" Rydell asked.

"I'll watch the rest of the room."

"Would you please explain to me why you want to kill me?" Banks asked in a voice loud enough for the whole room to hear.

"You killed someone I knew," Moffat growled.

"Who, pray tell? I've killed no one as ugly as you, friend."

Banks was trying to rile Moffat to the point he might make a mistake that would give the killer the edge, but the Faraday man was more than a little experienced and knew what Banks was up to. Moffat asked, "You going to die sitting down or standing up?"

"I'm not going to die today at all, my friend," Banks said carefully. "You, on the other hand, might not be so lucky."

Linc noticed something different in the killer's expression, then noted the man's left hand under the table. "Harley, let it go."

Moffat never took his eyes off the killer. "What?"

Linc moved forward. "He knows, Harley. He knew who you were the moment you walked in here."

"What are you going on about, Linc?"

"Look at his left hand."

Moffat checked it and realized Linc had just saved his life.

"You going to back up the words you're spouting or what?" Banks goaded.

Moffat stared at the killer. His whole body trembled with rage. Here in front of him was the arrogant man he wanted to kill more than any other, and he couldn't do it because Banks more than likely had a gun pointed at him under the table.

"Walk away, Harley," Linc said in a low voice. "There'll be another time."

"He killed my wife, Linc."

"I know, Harley. I know."

Moffat's shoulders slumped, and he turned away from the grinning killer. He walked toward the doors while his friends watched his back.

Once they were outside, Linc caught up with him. "You all right, Harley?"

Moffat looked up at him, and Linc could see the distress in the other man's eyes. "He killed her, and I need to make it right. I've been one step behind him all the time. Every time I find out where he is, he's gone by the time I get there. Now he's here."

"I know. And when the time comes, I'll help you get it done. I promise you that."

* * *

"What happened?" Faraday asked as he stood on the verandah outside the Cottage.

Linc stopped while the others walked past him. "Banks was ready. I managed to convince Harley it wasn't the time."

The agency owner nodded. "Figures."

"You knew this would happen, didn't you?" Linc said.

"I thought it would give Harley a chance to square the ledger."

"It nearly got him killed."

"It didn't, though, did it?"

Linc's gaze hardened. "It damned well could have. If I hadn't been there, you'd be burying him."

"It's a good thing you were then, isn't it?" Faraday said. "Now that you've got that off your chest, I've got something else for you to do."

"What?"

"I need you to send a telegram to St. Louis. McCoy wants to put on a little show there as we pass through. A man called Charles Bishop looks after the stockyards at the railroad station. We need the use of the yards."

"Okay."

"Do it now."

"I'll take care of it."

"Thanks."

Chapter 14

A little after noon two days later, the buffalo train rolled into Abilene. There was no fanfare, but word soon spread throughout the town, and a crowd gathered to look at the magnificent beasts from the plains.

"Get them unloaded and into the yards where they can be fed and watered," Creed ordered.

Looking around, he saw Matthew Faraday approaching, which surprised him. Linc Peters was with Faraday, too, so Creed knew something was wrong. He shook hands with Faraday and asked, "What's happening?"

"I'll tell you later. How did it go?"

"Nothing we couldn't handle."

Creed looked at Linc. "You here to ride shotgun on the train?"

He nodded. "Something like that. Me, Harley Moffat, Rydell, and French."

Creed remembered something. "Has Harley seen—"

"Yes."

"What happened?"

"I'll fill you in later," Linc said.

"Seems to be a lot of that going around." Creed shook his head and rubbed his chin.

Liza Joined them, and Creed introduced her to Faraday and Linc. Before they could discuss anything else, they were interrupted.

"You're under arrest, Creed," a voice said loudly from outside the group. "I've rode a long way to do this."

Creed turned slightly as the crowd parted to reveal Jack Theron, along with Tyrone, Willy, and Mason. "You being funny, Jack?" Creed asked.

"Nothing funny about murder."

"Who did I murder?"

"Lucky is who."

The Texan snorted. "He was strung up all proper and legal, Jack."

"He was murdered," Jack Theron insisted with a hate-filled snarl twisting his face.

Faraday moved away, taking Liza by the arm. He said, "This is no place for us, miss. Step over here with me."

Linc Peters stepped up beside Creed, and as he did, the other Faraday men strode up and moved into position as well. Linc and Moffat were to Creed's right, while Rydell and French were on his left.

Jack frowned. "What the hell are they?"

"Friends of mine, Jack."

"This don't have a damn thing to do with them, Creed."

"It does now," Linc said. "You threaten one Faraday man, you threaten all of us."

"You mind if we deal ourselves in on this one?" Rio Wade asked as he moved up beside Jack Theron and the other men from Glory. Behind him came Slim, Kent, and the fourth man of the gang, Jones. "I reckon this kind of evens the numbers up a little."

"You don't want to do this," Creed said, his voice loud and clear enough to be heard by everyone in the street, where a hush of anticipation had fallen. "There's no need for anyone to die here."

"Too late," Jack Theron stated. "Somebody already has."

From beside the Texan, Linc said, tight-lipped, "They killed Yates."

Creed's jaw firmed, but his hand didn't move until Jack Theron abruptly clawed for the gun on his hip.

Then Creed's hand flashed to his own Colt.

The slug that erupted from Creed's gun a shaved fraction of a second later punched into Jack Theron's chest before Jack even cleared leather. The second bullet slammed less than an inch to the left of the first, and the crooked town marshal was out of the fight.

Beside Creed, Linc took down Tyrone. One shot, one kill. From then on, it became a wild melee of flying bullets and loud curses between the two groups of men as the citizens of Abilene scrambled to get out of the line of fire.

Rio Wade managed to get off at least one shot, which hit Briar French in the upper left arm and spun the agent around. Wade looked to get in a killing shot but was beaten to the punch when Rydell plugged one into his guts.

Wade doubled over and sank to his knees, his gun falling from his suddenly nerveless fingers.

Kent died when Linc put a bullet through his throat, and Slim, hell-bent on revenge for Creed shooting off his finger, got off one shot at the Texan. Despite his claims, he couldn't shoot very well with his left. He missed by a good foot, which gave Creed the opportunity to shoot him in the head.

Harley Moffat stood amid all the flying lead and accounted for the last two Therons, Willy, the youngest brother, and cousin Mason. Both died grisly deaths, taking a charge of buckshot at close range from Moffat's cut-down shotgun.

As abruptly as it began, it was over. The echoes of the shots rolled across the plains, and what had been a violent and bloody shootout was done.

Creed looked around at the fallen men until his eyes came to rest on Rio Wade. The killer was hunched over, his arms wrapped across the front of his body, cradling his abdomen against the burning pain starting to filter through it.

The Texan walked over to him, and Wade looked up at him. Agony filled his eyes. "I guess I'm d-done."

Creed nodded. "I guess you are."

"F-funny, I never thought I...I'd get through the War alive. But I did...until now..."

"Did you and Miles steal the Kelly herd? Are you responsible for the deaths of Max Kelly and all those other cowboys?"

Wade looked at him kind of funny and gave a wry

smile. Just when the Texan thought he was about to admit to the crimes, he fell forward and died. One corner of Creed's mouth quirked in disappointment.

"Briar, you all right?"

That question prompted Creed to turn and check on his allies. He saw Rydell walk over to the wounded Briar French, who muttered something inaudible. Creed felt a presence beside him and saw Liza Kelly standing there, her face pale.

"That was...wild," she said, her throat sounding dry.

"It was," Creed replied. "Are you all right?"

"Me? I'm fine. Just a little shook up. I reckon he is too." She nodded at Hank Miles, who stood grim-faced on the boardwalk, astonished at the carnage before him.

Beside Miles was Banks, who seemed mildly amused by what he'd just witnessed.

"What do you figure he's going to do?" Liza asked Creed. "He just lost most of his men."

"I don't know," Creed said. "But I've got a hunch he's not done making trouble for us yet."

* * *

Miles was more than a little shaken. Everything he was working toward was falling apart around him; the gunfight had been the biggest blow so far. He sat at a table in a back room at the Longhorn, a half-empty bottle before him. As he poured another shot of whiskey, his hand trembled with anger, the bottle hitting the edge of the glass with a tinkling sound that echoed through the room.

When the door opened, he looked up and saw Banks enter the room. He sneered at the killer. "I didn't see you trying to help out there today, Banks. Some hired killer you turned out to be."

Banks sat at the table. "So, you're sitting in here feeling sorry for yourself, are you?"

"What do you want?"

"What are your plans?" the assassin asked in a low voice.

"They haven't changed."

"Who is your man in St. Louis?"

"Why?"

"I've decided to help out."

"Now you decide," Miles said bitterly.

"Who is your man?"

"Barney Gibbs. Do you know him?"

Banks nodded. "Did some work for him once. There's a train coming through later today. I'll be on it."

"What if you don't succeed?" Miles asked.

"Then I'll do it in Chicago."

Miles stared at him for a moment and said, "I'm coming with you. Consider yourself on our payroll."

"*Our* payroll?"

"You don't think all this money is mine, do you? I'm coming."

Banks shrugged. "Suit yourself."

* * *

McCoy looked a lot better, even if he was still bedridden. He smiled at Creed. "Am I glad to see you! They tell me you've got some buffalo."

"We have three, and we're holding them in the yards until it's time," Creed said, taking the man's offered hand. "The boys did all the work."

McCoy nodded and looked at Faraday. "I have a safe downstairs. Would you ask Sally to open it for you and pay them for me?"

Faraday nodded. "I can do that."

"What was all the shooting a little while ago? Letting off a bit of steam, huh?"

"Not quite." Faraday told him what had happened.

"I'm glad everyone is fine, but Miles isn't going to take this lying down."

"You let us worry about him," the agency owner stated.

"When are you leaving for St. Louis?" McCoy asked Creed.

"Tomorrow."

McCoy shook his head. "No, the train won't be ready by then."

Creed frowned. "What do you mean?"

"Streamers have to be attached, and signs have to be painted. We need this to be eye-catching. We have to draw attention to it—the press's attention."

"Damn it, Joe," Faraday growled. "This isn't a damned circus."

"That's exactly what it is, Matt. Exactly." He turned his gaze to Creed. "We're going to need three of the best ropers you can find."

"You'll need more than three," Creed told him.

"Also, some unbroke horses."

"What?"

191

"We'll rope them too."

"Why don't we find some elk while we're at it?" Faraday asked with an exasperated expression on his face.

McCoy's eyes widened. "Yes, yes. Fantastic suggestion. Get me a couple of those as well." The man was smiling at the prospect of the spectacle it would be, his enthusiasm only slightly dampened because he might not have been around to see it.

"Me and my big mouth," the agency owner growled. He looked at Creed. "Well, what are you waiting for? You've got your orders."

* * *

"Miles left on the train this afternoon," Jack Hawk said to Creed as he sat down beside Liza at the table in the Drover's Cottage. "Banks went with him."

Creed nodded.

"What does that mean?" Liza asked.

"It means it isn't over, just like I thought," the Texan replied.

Linc fingered his glass of whiskey. "Harley ain't gonna be happy."

"He rode out not long after the train left," Hawk told him.

"Damn it," Linc growled. "I'm going to have to tell Matt."

Rising from his seat, he moved away from the table and walked off.

"What's all that about?" Liza asked.

"Banks killed Moffat's wife a few years back,"

Creed said, his face a grim mask.

"Good Lord," Liza gasped.

"I picked the best of the hands to be ropers for the buffalo," Hawk said, changing the subject.

"Are you counting yourself as one of them, Jack?" Liza asked.

Hawk made a disgusted face. "No, I had enough of trying to rope those locomotives on hooves the first time around."

"But you're good, Jack. One of the best."

"Miss Liza, there's a difference between being good and being crazy. I prefer to remain firmly in the first category."

"All right," said Creed. "You're going to love this, then."

"Is it worse than putting streamers on the stock cars?"

"McCoy wants a couple of elk and some wild horses to go with the buffalo."

Hawk stared at Creed for a moment, then smiled and shook his finger at him, thinking the Texan had to be playing a joke on him.

"Ha, good one. For a second there, I thought you said 'elk.'"

"I did."

Hawk groaned. "They'll have to be females. No way we can throw a rope over a full head of antlers."

"He didn't say what they had to be."

"Hell and damnation," Hawk said. "This whole mess is getting out of control."

Creed smiled. "I knew I could count on you."

"How soon do you need them?"

"As soon as you can get them here."

* * *

Liza snuggled into Creed's side. The sun shone through the hotel room window and bathed them with its warmth. Their lovemaking had lasted long into the night, and in the early morning, after talking for an hour, they'd drifted off to sleep.

Creed stroked her back lightly with his fingers, and she began to stir. He brushed the hair off her face, and she smiled without opening her eyes. "Morning."

"Good morning to you too," he replied.

"That sun feels good."

"It sure does."

Liza reached up and traced a finger down his chest through the thick mat of hair. Before she could do anything else, a loud knock sounded on the door.

"Creed, you awake?"

The Texan's eyes widened at the sound of Faraday's voice. "Blast, what does he want?"

"Come on, John, I know you're in there," Faraday persisted.

"Might as well open the door," Liza told Creed. "I don't think he's going away."

With a grumble, Creed climbed out of bed and pulled his pants on, then walked to the door and opened it a crack. "What is it?"

"I have a job for you," Faraday declared. As always, no matter what the time or situation, he was as well-dressed and looked cool and steady.

"What?"

"Open the damned door and let me in, will you?"

Creed swung the door back. Faraday walked in and stopped short when he saw Liza with a sheet pulled up around her. "Oh, I'm interrupting."

"A minute later and you might have been," Liza told him, smiling.

Faraday looked even more uncomfortable. "Can I have a word in the hall, John?"

He turned and retreated from the room. Creed glared at Liza, who beamed at him. He followed his boss into the hallway and asked, "What's up?"

"I want you to go after Harley."

Creed frowned. "We don't even know where he's gone."

"St. Louis."

"How—"

"Because that's where Banks and Miles bought tickets to."

"What do you want me to do when I find him?"

"Stop him from getting killed, at least until we get there. I think we'll be ready to leave with the train the day after tomorrow."

"You think?"

"We'll be ready by then unless McCoy decides he wants damned elephants or something else to take with him."

"Well—"

"Don't say it," Faraday warned, holding up an admonishing finger.

"I'll leave this morning," Creed said. He might complain, but he didn't want anything happening to Harley Moffat. The frontiersman was a friend as well as an excellent operative. Face to face, Moffat was a match for Rudy Banks, but the assassin couldn't be counted on to fight fair.

"Good man," Faraday said, nodding. "You'll need to ride over to Junction City and get a train from there. There's not one coming through here until late tomorrow. Just be careful."

* * *

Hank Miles sat at the cloth-covered table and patted his mouth with a napkin. He looked up from his lunchtime meal and said, "Delicious."

Barney Gibbs smiled. "That it was. Don't you think so, Mr. Banks?"

Banks shrugged. "It was food, I guess. I've had better in New York restaurants."

Gibbs chuckled. "I like an honest man."

"Like you, I'm far from it."

Gibbs chuckled again and looked at Miles. "See? An honest man, whether he wants to admit it or not. Now, Mr. Miles, let's discuss business. What do you want from me?"

Miles filled him in on his problem and the desired outcome. Once he was finished, Gibbs nodded and said, "That ought to be easy enough to accomplish."

"How much?"

"What's it worth to you?"

"I'll pay you ten thousand for your help."

Gibbs nodded thoughtfully, steepling his fingers in front of his face. "Agreed."

A waiter in a black suit approached the table,

leaned down, and spoke quietly into Gibbs' ear. He then walked away, leaving them to finish their meals. Gibbs said, "It seems we have another problem to deal with."

* * *

The door of the abandoned house swung open, admitting the group of five men. "We have him in the living room, sir," the man who'd led them there said.

The inside smelled musty and damp, and with each footstep, the floorboards creaked. Wallpaper peeled off the walls, and pieces of the ceiling had fallen to the floor. What had once been a fancy house was now dilapidated, most of it in serious need of repair. They walked into the old living room and found two men standing guard over another who was tied to a chair.

Crossing the room to stand in front of the seated individual, the man who had guided them into the house said, "We found him following our guests."

Miles looked at Gibbs. "You had your men following us?"

"I trust no one," Gibbs said. "Whether I know them or not. Do you know him?"

Miles shook his head. "Hard to tell."

Banks stepped forward, grabbed a handful of hair, and lifted the head so they could see the prisoner's face. A cut above the left eye had caused blood to cover that side of his face. The eye was all but closed, and the right one wasn't far behind it. The man's nose was broken, and there was a deep gash on his right cheek.

The killer nodded. "I know him. Was he carrying anything?"

The man who had led them here dug in his pocket. He retrieved something that glinted in the lamplight and tossed it to Banks, who caught it, then looked down at the badge that read *Faraday Security Service*.

The killer turned his head to look at Gibbs. "What plans do you have for him?"

"I'm not sure. Why?"

"Leave it to me, and I'll make the problem go away for you." An evil grin crossed the assassin's lips.

Apart from the look on Banks' face, there was something else about the man that made Gibbs' blood run cold. He shrugged and said, "Why not? He's all yours."

* * *

St. Louis was a big place, and Creed had no idea where to begin his search for Harley Moffat if he was even in the city. With no clues pointing to the agent's whereabouts, he could wander aimlessly, wasting time that Harley might not have. He needed a starting point, and that meant locating someone who had their finger on the pulse of the city.

There was only one place for him to go.

The burgeoning clouds above opened, releasing their contents on the city as he approached the front door of a Lafayette Square-style house. A broad man in a suit blocked his path and gave him a stern stare. Creed said, "I've come to see O'Halloran."

"Mr. O'Halloran doesn't want to see you."

"Tell him John Creed is here to see him."

"I don't care if you're the president. I'm not letting you in," the man growled.

"I'm asking nicely, my friend," Creed told him. "Don't make me lose my manners."

The man just stood there with his arms folded.

Creed sighed and reached into his pocket to pull out his badge. "I work for the Faraday Security Service."

"Never heard of them," the man lied.

"I'm getting wet here, friend," Creed said as rainwater dripped from the brim of his hat.

"So?"

Creed's right hand streaked outward and his arm straightened. The hard fist crashed into the man's jaw, dropping him like a stone. The Texan looked down at the unconscious man. "Now look what you made me go and do. Don't say I didn't warn you."

Creed dropped his badge into his pocket and brushed his hands off as he looked around to see if anyone had witnessed the assault. Then he opened the door and walked into a large foyer. It was vacant, and not wanting to be taken for an intruder, he called, "Hey, anybody home?"

He waited for a moment, then heard footsteps. A man in a suit appeared. He frowned at Creed and asked, "Who are you?"

"Creed. I'm here to see O'Halloran."

"How'd you get past Toby?"

"Walked."

The man looked at the door.

"He's all right," Creed said. "Just having a nap. Don't worry, he's out of the rain."

"You've got a lot of nerve, Creed."

"Just want to see the man, and I'll be on my way."

A door opened off the foyer, and a second well-dressed, thick-set man appeared. "What the hell is going on?" he asked in a heavy Irish accent.

"I gather you're O'Halloran?" Creed asked.

"What if I am? Who are you?"

"I'm John Creed. I work for the Faraday Security Service."

"A dirty stinking copper, are you?"

"A private detective, actually. We mainly work for the railroads."

"I haven't robbed no trains lately, Creed. Now shove off."

Creed nodded. "I appreciate that, but that's not the reason I'm here. I'm looking for information."

O'Halloran snorted derisively. "Shove off, I said."

"I'm looking for a man, a friend of mine. He came to St. Louis maybe the day before yesterday. I'm not sure."

"That tells me absolutely nothing."

"He's here to kill the Man in Black."

That got O'Halloran's attention. His bushy eyebrows rose as he asked, "Banks? Banks is in St. Louis?"

"Yes. Came here with a man named Miles."

"Rudy Banks?"

"Yes, Rudy Banks."

"That explains the body they found on my patch

this morning."

Creed's blood ran cold.

"A body was found in an alley behind Dorian and Sons Furniture Builders," O'Halloran went on. "All cut up and not pretty. Now the coppers are looking at me because it was on my patch."

"I take it you had nothing to do with it?"

"Of course not." O'Halloran snorted. "I'm an honest businessman, don't you know."

"Where did they take the body?"

"Downtown."

"You don't know who he was?"

O'Halloran shook his head. "If I knew, I'd have said, wouldn't I?"

"Thanks for your time," Creed said and turned to walk back out.

"Wait, why is Banks in town?"

"Relax. I doubt he's here for you."

"How can you be sure?"

"You're still alive, aren't you?" Creed replied.

* * *

Moffat was a mess. Banks had worked him over so thoroughly that he was almost unrecognizable. It was only the badge found with his body that provided a positive identification.

Creed looked at Binns, the policeman who stood beside the corpse in the local morgue. "That's him. What happened?"

"He was found in an alley. Whoever did that to him was a damned butcher. You have any idea who it might have been?"

"No idea," Creed lied. "Can you tell me how to get to where he was found?"

"Sure."

The policeman gave him the details and left the room. Creed looked at the disfigured corpse once more and let the image burn itself into his brain before he too turned and left.

* * *

The alley was poorly lit due to the high walls of the buildings on either side. It stank of human waste, and he guessed that it was a haven at night for those who had nowhere else to go. He looked around to try to find anything that might be a lead, but he knew it was probably a lost cause. Then he saw a man wearing not much more than rags shuffling along the alley toward him.

Creed approached him cautiously, but as soon as the man noticed him, he started to walk away.

"Wait," Creed called. "I want to talk to you."

The man shuffled faster.

"I'll give you money."

The man stopped. Turned. "Money?"

"That's right. But first, I want some questions answered."

"What questions?"

Closer now, Creed could see his face more clearly. He was dirty, unshaven, and smelled like a dog that had been dead for a week. "Do you sleep here at night?"

"Yes, sometimes."

"Were you here last night?"

The man looked at the ground. "No."

"What's your name?"

"Peter."

"I'm John."

"Uh-huh."

Creed tried again. "Were you here last night, Peter?"

"No."

"All right," Creed said. "If you're sure." He turned to walk away.

Peter took a tentative step after him. "Hey, wait, what about the money?"

"I said I'd give you some if you answered the questions."

Peter nodded. "I did."

"Not the ones I wanted answered."

"What ones?"

"Were you here last night?"

"No."

Creed started to walk.

"All right, all right, yes. I was here." Peter's voice was anguished.

"Were you here when the body was brought here?"

"I can't answer that."

"Why not?" Creed asked.

"They'll kill me."

"So, you were here. Did you see who it was?"

The man's voice was hoarse. "Please, mister, don't make me answer that."

"Tell me this then," Creed said. "Was it O'Halloran?"

"No, it wasn't his men."

"Olsen?"

"No."

"Gibbs?"

"I can't answer that."

"So, it *was* Gibbs."

"I didn't say that," Peter responded with a fearful note in his voice.

Creed dug into his pocket. "It's fine, Peter. It's fine."

* * *

McCoy struggled down the stairs and went outside to watch the men put the finishing touches on the train. "It looks good," he told Faraday.

"It looks like a traveling circus if you ask me."

"Yes, but it'll gain attention, which is exactly what I need. Are the animals ready?"

Faraday grunted. "Yes. Three buffalo, three wild mustangs, and a couple of elk. Is there anything else?" He muttered under his breath, "Heaven help us if there is."

"No, I don't think so."

"Thank—"

They turned as shouts came from across the tracks at the corrals. With a crash, the fence shattered and a young buffalo bull emerged, throwing his head around and pawing the ground.

Faraday groaned. "Damn it!"

Four cowboys appeared, whirling lariats as they tried to rope the angry beast before he could take off for the tall and uncut plains. The animal sharply turned on one of the cowboys and lowered his head, then charged. There was a sickening thud as the beast hit the young Texan, knocking him back about ten feet.

McCoy watched, stunned at the violence. The buffalo hit the prone cowboy again, fifteen hundred pounds of enraged animal doing its best to kill the man.

The shouts grew louder before one of the other men managed to get a rope on the beast, then a second and a third. Finally, they had the animal under control, and another cowboy succeeded in dragging the downed Texan away from the wild-eyed animal.

Surprisingly, the cowboy seemed not much the worse for wear. He limped a little as he walked off, but that was it. He'd been a very lucky man.

Faraday turned to McCoy. "I hope this is damned well worth it, Joe."

McCoy gave him a nervous smile. "Me, too."

Faraday saw Linc approaching them with a concerned expression on his face. He carried a piece of paper in his hand, and the agency owner could only assume it was bad news.

"How bad is it, Linc?" Faraday asked.

"Harley's dead, Matt. Creed says so right here in this telegram."

Faraday felt a surge of anger flow through him. "Was it Banks?"

"Looks that way."

"What's Creed doing about it?"

Linc shrugged. "Whatever he can, I guess."

"This is my fault," Faraday said.

"Harley was a big boy. He knew what he was doing."

"That doesn't make me feel any better."

"It wasn't meant to," Linc said.

Chapter 15

The establishment was called the St. Louis Stag. It was a gentlemen's club that catered to the well-to-do, which was probably why Creed was stopped at the front desk and barred from proceeding any farther.

"You can't go in there dressed like that, sir," the desk clerk said, sniffing as he looked him up and down.

"I'm looking for Barney Gibbs," Creed stated again. "I know he's here."

"That may be so, sir, but like I said, you can't come in."

The Texan eyed the rat-faced clerk, and for a fleeting moment, he thought about leaving. Then he asked. "What do I need to get in there?"

"A tie and a jacket."

"Is that it?"

"Yes, sir."

Creed looked around the foyer and saw the guard standing at the door. He gave the clerk a smile and said, "I'll be right back."

Walking over to the bearded man, who stood ramrod-straight outside the door, he said, "Can I borrow your jacket and tie?"

The man frowned. "Go away."

"You sure I can't?"

"Go away."

Creed moved fast. His left hand streaked out, and his knuckles hit the man in the throat, stunning him. The man staggered and the Texan hit him again, this time in the middle, doubling him over. While he gasped for air, Creed helped him out of his jacket and then relieved him of his tie. The clerk stood watching, mouth agape.

Creed shrugged into the guard's coat and had his tie loosely done up around his throat. "Not the best of fits, but it'll do." He opened the door to the main room of the gentlemen's club and walked in.

It was the epitome of grandeur—polished timber paneling on the walls and twin chandeliers on the ceiling, surrounded by plaster roses. The strong scents of cigar smoke and stale alcohol permeated the stuffy room. Large paintings of naked ladies adorned the walls, illuminated by wall sconces beside them. None of the art came close to the real things walking around in frilly undergarments with their top halves bare as they served the customers in more ways than one.

One of the women approached Creed, an amply-endowed blonde with heavy rouge on her face. "You lost, cowboy?"

"Looking for someone."

"Me, I hope." She gave him a dazzling but

professional smile.

"Maybe another time," he replied.

She looked disappointed. "Who are you looking for, Tex?"

"Barney Gibbs."

She nodded in the direction of four men who sat below a large painting where the lamp cast a good light on them. Creed nodded. "Appreciate the help, ma'am."

She reached out and touched his arm. "If you're looking for some sport later, I'll be around."

She walked off, wiggling her behind as she went, then moved toward a group of three older men. One reached up and pulled her onto his lap. Creed heard a playful shriek escape her lips.

When told he'd find Gibbs at the gentlemen's club, his immediate thought had been of a quiet, dignified place where men sat drinking and smoking cigars. A place where they could mingle among their own without wives interrupting whatever it was they did. Well, he'd been wrong on that score. Almost certainly, no wives were here, but the place was far from quiet and dignified.

Creed started toward the table where Gibbs sat talking with three men. One of them looked up and saw his approach. Creed saw him reach under his suit coat and leave his hand there.

Gibbs observed his man's reaction and looked up. His eyes locked onto Creed, and he leaned back in his seat. When the Texan stopped, the gangster asked, "Why is a poor excuse for a gentleman like you standing before me?"

"You Gibbs?"

"Mr. Gibbs to trash like you." He sneered. "Listen, I don't have the time nor the inclination to be talking to you. Now, get lost before I let Craig throw you out."

"I came here prepared to do this respectful-like, and there you go, being all uppity. I guess all that power you think you wield has gone to your head."

Anger flushed Gibbs' face, its color changing to crimson. The man on his left spluttered in a heavy English accent, "I say, old chap, there's no call to be uncivil."

"I say, old chap," Creed replied mockingly, "shut the hell up."

Gibbs glared at him and motioned for his man Craig to deal with the situation.

Creed said to Gibbs' henchman, "Friend—and I use that term loosely—if you so much as move, I'm going to pull my Colt and punch your ticket permanently."

Craig looked at his boss for guidance. Gibbs held out a hand, and the tough relaxed a little. Gibbs' eyes narrowed and the sneer remained on his face as he said, "Let's hear what he wants before he gets buried."

The Englishman stood up. "I'll leave you to talk business."

Creed looked at the other man, who was still seated. "You, too. This don't concern you."

Seemingly relieved, the round-faced man struggled to his feet and hurried away. The Texan focused his attention on Gibbs and Craig.

"Well?" asked Gibbs. "Let's start with your name,

then we can proceed to the details of what you want."

"The name's Creed. A friend of mine turned up dead in an alley behind a furniture factory. I want to know what *you* know about it."

"I know nothing," Gibbs replied. He looked at Craig. "You?"

"No, sir," Craig said with a shake of his head.

"All I want to know is where I can find the man who did it."

"Don't know what you mean," Gibbs said blandly.

"Banks. It's his work. No one else is that much of an animal."

"Never heard of him." Gibbs smiled smugly. "And I don't know anything about your dead friend."

"Your men were seen dumping the body. I'm sure O'Halloran would be interested to know who brought the police onto his patch, as he calls it."

"If you think I'm scared of that Mick, you're sadly mistaken."

Creed was getting nowhere fast, and apart from using violence, he was unsure of how to get the information he needed. Maybe what he was doing would be enough. Hopefully Gibbs would let on to someone that he was here, and Banks would come after him. On the other hand, it could go the opposite direction, and Gibbs could send a heap of his own men after him.

"Tell Banks I'm looking for him," Creed said and turned to leave.

Gibbs said, "You just buried yourself, Creed."

* * *

"You brought this problem to my doorstep, now get rid of it," Barney Gibbs snarled at Banks. "I mean it. I want it gone."

Banks nodded placatingly. "I'll take care of it soon enough. First, we need to deal with the other matter."

"What other matter?"

"The train, of course. It should be arriving any day now."

Gibbs grunted angrily. "What's your plan for it?"

"Let the buffalo out, and in the confusion, kill McCoy."

"Is that it?"

"Yes."

"You make it sound so simple."

Banks nodded. "It will be if it all goes to plan."

"What do you mean, 'if?'"

"Things have a way of changing at the last moment." The smile on Banks's face sent a chill through Gibbs. "But I know how to cope with the unexpected."

* * *

Creed considered the problem long and hard before coming to a decision. If it worked, it would be like replacing one snake with another. Not that the second snake didn't already exist, but it would give him more power. When he looked at the bigger picture, he knew his wasn't the best option, but it far outweighed anything else he'd been able to think of.

The Texan nodded and said with a smile,

"O'Halloran, how would you like to gain control of an additional third of St. Louis?"

* * *

Linc walked along the side of the train, checking to make sure everything was ready to go. It had taken longer than they anticipated, but everything was done; the cars were decorated, the animals were securely aboard, and passengers were ready to leave. He looked up and saw Faraday waiting for him.

"Are we ready?"

Linc nodded. "As we'll ever be. Have you heard any more from Creed?"

Faraday shook his head. "Not since I got the word about Harley."

"So, we could be riding a train to Hell as far as we know," Linc said.

"Look at it this way," Faraday said. "It'll add to the surprise."

"Just what I need. More surprises."

"Excuse me, Mr. Faraday."

Faraday turned to see the telegraph operator standing patiently with a piece of paper in his hand. "Yes?"

"A telegram from Washington, sir."

Faraday took it and began to read. The telegrapher turned to leave, but the agency owner said, "Wait."

When he was finished reading, his gaze hardened as he stared at the telegrapher. "If word of this gets back to Miles—"

"I beg your pardon, sir?"

"Don't give me that. I know you feed him information. Understand this: if any part of the message I've just read gets back to Miles, I'm going to have one of my men take you three days out into the middle of Kiowa territory and set you afoot. Do you understand?"

"Y-yes, sir, Mr. Faraday." The man swallowed hard.

"Good."

* * *

Gibbs wasn't satisfied with the answers given by Banks. Creed had slighted him, and the damned Texan would pay. He'd worry about the train later, Gibbs decided. He sent some of his men to fix the problem.

They were led by Tobe Johnson, a New Yorker who had provided a particular service for a man named Isiah White when he was an up-and-comer in the war for the docks.

After the fighting between the North and South ended, men came home and found what little they'd had had simply vanished. Some drifted west, and others lived on the street, but not White. He saw that there was money to be made by controlling the docks. A dollar here, a death there, and he soon had his small waterfront empire. Tobe Johnson had been a big part of it.

That was, however, before he erred by killing the wrong person and had a bounty of five thousand dollars placed on his head. That brought unwanted attention to White, so he sent his man to St. Louis to work for an old friend. White's loss had been Gibbs' gain.

While Craig was Gibbs' personal muscle, Johnson was his troubleshooter. And here he was troubleshooting a problem once again.

There were five of them, dressed in black suits covered by long coats that reached their knees. Each man had a hand in a bottomless pocket, where they grasped hidden sawed-off coach guns. They walked purposefully into the foyer of the hotel where Creed was staying. The clerk saw them on approach, and rather than try to be a hero, he resignedly turned the register so Johnson could read it.

The killer pointed at a name on the register and looked up. "Is he in his room?"

With a jerky shake of his head, the clerk said, "He...he's in the dining room."

Without further ado, the five men moved toward the dining room, leaving the clerk staring nervously after them.

When they entered, Johnson saw that the room was more than half full of patrons enjoying their meals. He called in a loud voice, "If your name isn't Creed, get out now."

A flurry of complaints was directed at him from more than a few customers. He raised his right hand, which caused the flap of his coat to slide away and reveal the shotgun. "Now," he repeated.

Amidst a clatter of silverware on plates, a flood of people swept toward the exits, leaving a lone figure sitting toward the back of the room at a solid-looking table. The five men began fanning out across the dining room. Johnson stepped forward a few paces before stopping.

"You're Creed, I take it."

"It would appear that way as I'm the only one left here," the Texan said, wiping his mouth with the linen napkin before placing it on the table.

"You're pretty calm for someone who's about to die."

"You seem confident you're going to kill me."

"Confidence don't enter into it."

"I think it does," Creed said. "I think what you are is over-confident. If you weren't, you would have noticed several things on your way in here."

Johnson raised his eyebrows. "Really? Do tell."

"The two new doormen, and the buggy across the street with the two men talking behind it. The fact that the desk clerk is new and didn't even question your reasons for five men looking for one customer."

Johnson cocked his head to one side with a confused expression on his face.

"Now," Creed continued, "if you care to look behind you, you'll see the desk clerk with a gun."

Johnson looked over his shoulder and chuckled. "You think he can take the five of us before we kill you both?"

The Texan shook his head. "No, I suspect not. However—"

The two side doors of the large dining room opened, and four more men entered. All were carrying weapons. Johnson's men started to mill around, raising their weapons against the sudden additional threat. By the time Gibbs' troubleshooter realized what was happening, Creed had his Yellow Boy above the table and pointed at Johnson's middle.

"You want to take a little extra time to think about your next decision?" Creed asked him.

This wasn't the way it was supposed to go, and Johnson was getting angrier with every heartbeat. His eyes narrowed, and a tic started in the corner of his left eye. Creed knew that this wasn't going to end well. The killer was about to do something stupid, and in a room full of flying buckshot wasn't the ideal place to be. He made the call and dropped the hammer on the Winchester.

The .44-caliber slug punched into Johnson's chest, forcing him up onto his toes. He stumbled for a moment before bringing his feet to a standstill, then looked down at the growing patch of red on his shirt and lifted his head to stare at Creed. A wisp of blue-gray smoke rose from the barrel of the Yellow Boy, which was still pointed at Johnson although Creed hadn't levered a fresh round into the breach. The killer lost the light in his eyes and fell to the floor with a thud.

Creed ran his gaze over the four remaining men, who stood transfixed, stunned by the death of their leader. The Texan said, "Get the hell out of here."

Without wasting any time, they went.

Chapter 16

The following day, not long after noon, the Buffalo Train rolled into St. Louis. Waiting for it was a brass band and more than one hundred citizens. Creed was surprised by the turnout, but he guessed that word had reached the city, and they wanted to see what the fuss was about.

Liza stepped down off the train and into his arms. After a quick kiss, she asked, "How are you, John?"

"I'm good. How was the journey?"

"Uneventful. I'm sorry about your friend."

Creed nodded. "I didn't know him that well, but no man deserves to die the way he did."

"What have you done about it?" Faraday asked, coming up behind him.

Creed related the recent events, and Faraday asked, "What's been the response?"

"There hasn't been one."

"And you have no idea where Banks is or what they're up to?"

"Not a lick."

"I thought you would have dealt with the problem by now," Faraday said, frowning.

Creed sighed. "Can't deal with it if you can't find it. I pushed Gibbs, and all he did was send his men after me. It was lucky I had some help."

"A deal with the devil is what it is," Faraday growled. "There's something you should know. I received a telegram just before we left Abilene. When you told me about what happened with Miss Kelly's herd and the governor taking a hand in it for Miles, I started one of my Washington men looking into it. It seems our friend Miles, the governor of Kansas, and one other gentleman are all close friends. Before he came west, Miles spent most of his time in Washington in the employ of a Kansas senator by the name of Wesley, Kurt Wesley. From what my man could decipher, he has a lot of money and a healthy interest in the cattle business."

"Do you mean the senator is in this with Miles?" Liza asked.

"It would explain where Miles got all his money," Creed said. "It would take a lot to set up an operation like his. Buying a herd even at fifteen dollars a head takes substantial capital. Add to that all the money that had to be poured into Ellsworth, which means they need every head of cattle to go through there in order to make a profit. Abilene is a threat to that."

"Exactly," Faraday agreed. "And with Miles doing everything out in Kansas, Wesley can remain in the background and not worry."

"What do you propose we do about him?" Creed asked.

"I've made the decision to go back to Washington and look into it further," Faraday explained.

"You taking anyone with you?"

"I'll have men on hand should I need them. You just worry about getting this train to Chicago in one piece."

The buffalo were unloaded, along with the horses and the elk. They were kept separate from other animals that were also penned in the yards. While this was going on, bald, irascible Charlie Bishop appeared. "You Creed?" he asked the Texan.

"That's me."

"Matt said I'd find you over here. I'm Charlie Bishop."

Creed took his offered hand. "Pleased to meet you."

"I've set aside the largest yard, where you folks can put on your display tomorrow."

Creed nodded. "Thanks, but you need to be talking to Joe McCoy."

"Where will I find him?"

"Over there, leaning against the rail and watching the buffalo," Creed said, indicating where McCoy was.

Bishop touched his hat brim. "Obliged."

* * *

Wraiths slipped through the shadows, moving silently. A thin sliver of moon lit the sky, throwing negligible light upon the city below. A muffled thud the only signal that one of the Texas herders had been stopped from raising the alarm.

More of them appeared on the other side of the

yards and dealt with the man standing guard there, after which they converged on the gates so they could swing them open.

Harsh whispers fluctuated between the shadowy figures as they tried to work out which of them was going to drive the buffalo out of their yard.

In the end, a single man entered the yard and circled around them to the right. The heavy beasts watched him curiously, following his passage with sleepy eyes. He stepped forward and raised his hands. "Heeya! Git gone. Go on."

The three animals looked at the man but didn't move. "Will you hurry up!" another man said in a harsh whisper.

"If you think you can do better, then you do it."

"Damn it," the other man growled and entered the yard.

That was all it took for the buffalo to start moving. However, it wasn't the open gate that was their target. Three locomotives of fifteen hundred pounds each charged the newcomer. Before he knew it, they were on top of him.

A sickening crunch was followed by a high-pitched scream as bones broke under the crushing onslaught. Men on the outside scrambled to help their friend, but it was no use. The damage was done.

One of them took out a six-gun and began firing it into the air. Startled, the animals leaped away from the man they'd crushed and ran toward the opposite fence. They crashed into it, and the whole fence shook under the impact. They grunted wildly at the barrier before turning back as one the way they'd come and going out the open gate.

As the animals disappeared into the darkness, a voice was heard to say, "Get Kirk."

"He's dead. Leave him."

"Make sure."

A pistol shot was followed by, "I'm sure."

"Right, let's go."

* * *

"Creed, get up!"

The pounding on the door started out seemingly miles away, but as Creed rose through the layers of sleep, it came closer.

"What is it?" he growled.

"Get up, damn it. We got a problem."

"Linc?"

"Yes."

Creed started to get out of the bed. Beside him, Liza shifted. "What's wrong?"

"I don't know. Stay there."

He fumbled in the semi-dark until he found his clothes and managed to get dressed, then scooped up his rifle and met Linc in the lamp-lit hallway. "What's so urgent?"

"Someone let the buffalo out of the yards," Linc explained.

"What about the guards?"

"One of them was killed, and the other has a busted head."

"Damn it. Let's go."

* * *

Jack Hawk met them at the yards with the other cowboys. Some of them had saddled their horses and were ready to go. Creed asked, "Any idea where they are?"

"Getting reports of them over by the Missouri River."

"Could be worse, I guess. They could have gone toward the Mississippi. Get the riders out and see if they can locate them. We'll follow on foot. And be careful; those animals will be well and truly riled by now. I'm hoping we can get them back before they kill anyone."

"Anyone else, you mean," Hawk corrected.

Creed's head turned. "What do you mean?"

"You riders get out there," Hawk ordered. As they loped off, he said to Creed, "Come with me."

Linc and the Texan followed him into the stockyard. He carried a lantern, and when he reached the dead man, he held it up. It was a ghastly sight; the body was a bloody crumpled mess. Hawk said, "I'm guessing he was one of the ones who let them out."

"The buffalo made short work of him," Creed observed.

"Wait," Linc said. "Lower the lantern."

Hawk did as he was asked. "What are we looking at?" Creed asked.

"See it? There's a hole in his head."

"Looks all stomped on to me," Hawk said.

"I see it," said Creed. "They made sure he was dead."

"Tough. Get stomped on *and* shot."

"They made sure he wasn't going to talk," said Creed.

"Poor son of a bitch wouldn't have talked anyway," Link said.

Creed nodded. This body interested him, but they could investigate later. Right now, they had more pressing problems.

"Let's go find those buffalo."

* * *

The first one was easy to locate. He'd traveled only a short distance before breaking through a house fence, having found flowers to eat. The crashing of the wild beast had woken the owner and his wife, who looked in horror at the shaggy creature while it destroyed one of their carefully tended flower beds.

The cowboys arrived and began trying to rope the brute. That took care of any hope that the rest of the garden would survive. Between fifteen hundred pounds of buffalo and two cowboys on horses trying to rope it, the flowers didn't stand a chance.

The second animal had successfully destroyed no less than five fences and terrorized the owners of those houses before the cowboys brought it under control. They had the most trouble with the third one.

"Where is it?" Creed asked Hawk.

"You won't believe it. The ornery son of a bitch doubled back along another street and almost gave us the slip. When we thought he was cornered, he did the last thing we expected. He walked through a closed door and into a ladies' apparel store."

"Damn it," Creed exclaimed. "What do we do, dig him out? Wait? Or shoot it?"

Hawk said, "If we wait, he'll do more damage than he's already done. And we can't shoot him. I guess it leaves one option."

"Let's go have a look," Creed said resignedly. "This should be interesting."

* * *

The crash that emanated from inside the semi-dark store made Creed wince. "That didn't sound too good."

"We've been hearing stuff like that ever since we got here."

Creed ran his gaze over the large building. The glass windows displaying mannequins attired in a variety of stylish clothes were only just visible by the light cast by dimmed lamps while the store was closed. "I thought this was a ladies' clothes store?"

"It is," Rydell confirmed.

"Biggest damned store I ever saw."

"It's a department store, so it's a little bigger than your normal one."

"Means the big son of a bitch can do more damage too," Creed pointed out.

"There is that."

Creed shivered at the thought of going inside and getting cornered by the beast. He looked at the men with him and asked, "Who's coming with me?"

There was a long silence before a voice said, "I'll do it."

Creed looked at Briar French. He'd not noticed that the man had joined them, having been focused on the building before him. He shook his head. "Not this time, Briar. That arm of yours is still healing."

"I'll do it," Rydell said. "I've got nothing better to do."

Creed handed Linc his Winchester. "Just in case."

"We can still shoot it," Linc pointed out.

"No, McCoy would never forgive me."

The two men walked toward the front of the store. The door hung lopsided by one hinge, and there was a mostly dark opening where it had been.

"Wait," Linc called after them. He held out a lantern. "You might need this."

Rydell took the lantern and walked into the store first. The trail of destruction was clear. Displays had been knocked down and trampled. A cabinet had been smashed, and mannequins lay crushed. Creed asked in a whisper, "Can you see him?"

"Nope."

A crash sounded from farther back in the building and made both men jump. Loud grunts were followed by more crashes. "Sounds like he found something he doesn't like," Rydell said. "Maybe he thinks those people-shaped things are real, and he's trying to kill them."

"They're called mannequins. And if you ask me, looking at this place, I'd say there's not much about it that he *does* like."

They pushed on into the building, peering into

the shadows where the light wouldn't reach and expecting the demon from hell to come charging out at them at any time.

The crash of gunfire filled the room with a deafening roar. Creed felt the wind-rip of bullets close to his head and flung himself to the floor. Beside him, Rydell returned fire with a flurry of shots.

"What are you shooting at?" Creed shouted.

"I don't kn—"

Another burst of gunfire cut off his words and replaced them with a grunt. Rydell fell to the floor, dropping the lantern. The glass shattered, coal oil spilled on a dress, and the flames quickly took hold of the fabric. Creed began trying to slap them out as he said in a low voice, "Chad, are you all right?"

There was no response, and through the light cast by the growing flames, he could see the other security agent's eyes wide open in death.

A loud crash from the back of the building was followed by another. The building started to tremble, and Creed's eyes widened as he realized what was happening. He rolled violently to his left and all but threw himself out of the way of the runaway four-legged locomotive.

The buffalo snorted at him as he rumbled past and crashed into the front wall of the store. The building shook heavily under the impact. The beast shook his head and turned around. Although he had poor eyesight, the orange light of the flames caught his attention. The beast pawed the floor and dropped his head. With a couple of grunts, he charged again, this time plowing through the rapidly growing flames, singeing his hide as he went.

The stench of burnt hair filled the room, and Creed realized that things would only get worse from here. The animal was bound to become more terrified and tear what was left of the place apart.

Then there was the bushwhacker who had killed Chad Rydell.

Bent low, Creed moved to the right, trying not to get caught in the light of the fire. Another shot rang out, and the bullet drove into a wall somewhere behind Creed. He ducked as he kept moving. The fire was growing, and the heat was radiating through the room. Smoke billowed over the displays that hadn't been destroyed by the rampaging buffalo.

Toward the back of the building, the buffalo was now crashing about. Judging by the way the building was shaking, Creed thought the creature was butting the walls as his anxiety grew along with the heat and flames.

Another shot, and this time, the bullet cut closer. The Texan now knew where it came from because he saw the muzzle flash. Creed fired his Colt twice at the spurts of orange flame before moving toward a counter where he took shelter. More shots were fired, and the counter vibrated under the impact of each slug.

Creed rose and returned fire again before dropping back down. He'd triggered three more shots, which left one round in the wheel.

When the Texan rose again to fire his last round, he spotted a large dark shadow thundering toward him amid the crackle of the fire and the flickering orange light it cast. He threw himself to the right just before the buffalo smashed through the counter, sending splinters flying in every direction.

Bright lights flashed before Creed's eyes as his head hit the floor. Stunned by the impact, he tried to claw his way to his feet, but his knees were as far as he got. He shook his head to clear the cobwebs, then blinked several times to see if that would help.

Not far away, the fire was spreading rapidly, illuminating the room further. When Creed looked up, he made out a figure standing in front of him. It was a little fuzzy, but it was there. He shook his head again, and the picture became clearer.

It was Rudy Banks.

The killer raised the gun he had in his right hand. "You are a hard man to kill, Creed."

"You haven't succeeded yet."

In the hellish light of the blaze, Banks' thin lips curved in an arrogant smile.

It was like a locomotive barreled through with its throttle wide open. One second Banks was about to kill John Creed, and the next he was gone, riding the rails of death as the buffalo crashed into him. It lifted him off his feet and sent him through a nine-foot-tall wall of flames.

Creed blinked, uncertain of what he'd just witnessed. Then he climbed to his feet and got out before the building collapsed on top of him.

* * *

The sun rose over a pile of blackened rubble. Smoke still filtered from the smoldering wreck that had once been the ladies' apparel store. Liza stood beside Creed with her arm hooked through his as he waited, staring at the mess.

Linc came over. "They found Rydell."

"What about Banks?"

"No sign. They found the buffalo, though."

"McCoy's going to have a calf," Creed growled.

Linc stared at him.

"Too early?"

"For buffalo steaks, it is."

"What the hell happened?" McCoy shouted as he approached the three of them. "What happened here?"

"Someone let the buffalo out," Creed replied.

"What? How?"

"The usual way. They opened the damn gate."

"What were the men doing while all this was happening?" McCoy growled.

"One of them died," Linc said stoically. "The other will take a while to get back on his feet. We also lost one of our own."

McCoy's face fell. "Oh. I didn't know."

"That's not all," Creed said. "We got two of the buffalo back. The third is inside that building, dead."

"Oh, no. Who did it?"

"Banks was involved, so we can assume Miles and maybe Gibbs were, too."

"What happened to Banks?" McCoy asked.

"We're hoping he's in there."

Creed released himself from Liza's arm. She asked, "What are you doing?"

"My job."

"What do you mean?"

"I know," Linc said. "Let me get my shotgun, and I'll come with you."

"John—"

He looked at her.

"Be careful."

* * *

Creed was done playing by the rules. Too many people had died to be worrying about them now. His first port of call was O'Halloran. The guard on the door happened to be the one from the last visit. He started to pull a gun from beneath his coat, but Creed already had his out with the hammer eared back.

"I'm in no mood to be messing with you today. You tell O'Halloran I'm here to see him, or I'll put you on the express to Hell."

The man raised both his hands and nodded.

He walked through the front door, leaving it open, which Creed and Linc took as an invitation to follow him.

Once inside the foyer, they stopped and waited. Within moments, O'Halloran appeared. He took one look at the guns and said, "What the bloody hell is going on?"

"I thought you agreed to help me out, you Mick son of a bitch," Creed growled.

O'Halloran looked confused. "What do you mean? I did, didn't I?"

"One time. Last night, the buffalo were let

loose, and people were killed," Creed growled. He raised his Colt and pointed it at the Irishman. "You agreed to have men there in the shadows, watching. What happened?"

O'Halloran raised his hands. "Wait, it was nothing personal. It was business."

"What kind of damned business?"

"Barney and I came to an agreement."

"You mean, you sold me out to that bastard? What price, O'Halloran? What was worth the lives of two men?"

"Lafayette Park to the Mississippi, then along the river for twenty blocks."

"Son of a bitch," Creed grated.

"Like I said, it was business."

"Where will I find Gibbs?"

"He could be anywhere."

"Linc."

Linc moved the shotgun and squeezed the trigger. A barrel discharged with a loud roar, and a painting on the foyer's wall was torn apart by buckshot.

"All right! All right! I'll tell you what I know."

"I'm waiting," Creed prompted impatiently.

"Gibbs is possibly at his club."

Creed raised his eyebrows. "'Possibly?'"

O'Halloran nodded. "He'll be there. It's on Tribeck Street."

"How many men does he have?"

"Five or six."

Creed grunted and walked out the door with Linc on his heels.

Chapter 17

"How do you want to do this?" Linc asked Creed.

"We'll just walk in there and see what happens. We need answers to questions."

The club was a large sandstone and brick building that sat on the corner of Tribeck and Onslow. It had large twin doors made from dark hardwood with glass inlaid in the top half. A painted sign above the door read *Guns and Garters*, with a *Men Only* sign below it.

"Let's go in," Creed said.

They walked across the street, halting halfway to let a horse-drawn streetcar by. Once it had passed, they kept on and went up the steps to the doors. Inside, it was as fancy as the previous gentlemen's club Creed had visited, only this one came with extra perks from the looks of it. No sooner had they entered than they saw two scantily clad young women leading an older man up a wide flight of stairs.

The clerk at the counter saw them looking and

said, "Councilman Bender likes to get an early start on the day."

"He'll be getting more than an early start," Creed surmised out loud.

"Can I help you, gentlemen?"

"Looking for Barney Gibbs," the Texan said.

"Mr. Gibbs isn't in," the man lied, his hazel eyes giving him away as the words left his mouth.

"Friend," Linc said to him, "you should be mighty happy you don't play poker with a face like that."

"Huh?"

"Where's Barney Gibbs?"

"He's upstairs."

"Is he alone?" Creed asked.

The clerk shook his head. "No, he's with Peggy."

"Who's Peggy?"

"One of the hostesses who takes care of the customers."

"You mean, whores."

"Yes, sir. I guess I do."

"Give me the room number," Creed said.

"Sir, I—" the man started, but his face paled when Linc opened his coat to reveal the shotgun.

"I don't think my friend quite got that," he said.

"Fourth floor, room 408. You can't miss it because it's at the end of the hallway."

Creed nodded. "Thank you for your help."

They walked across the foyer toward the staircase. It was only wide as far as the first-floor landing, and from there, it was narrow up to the fourth floor.

Once they reached the final landing, the hallway led to the left and right. Creed checked which way the numbers ran and turned to his right. The clerk had been telling the truth about the room being at the end of the hall.

When they reached the door, Creed didn't bother knocking. He raised his foot and kicked it just below the lock. Wood splintered, and the door flew back and crashed against the wall. A sharp yelp emanated from within, the sound a startled woman would make. Linc went in first, his coach gun raised and ready to fire.

Creed followed close behind. The room was large, approximately three times the size of a normal room. It had luxurious drapes at the large windows, fine furniture, and an open fireplace with a polished mantel. To the left was a large bed, currently occupied by Barney Gibbs and his sporting woman.

"What the hell is this?" Gibbs screeched maniacally.

"Shut up and listen," Linc snapped.

Gibbs saw Creed and knew exactly what was happening. "You again."

"Yeah, me again."

The woman in the bed beside Gibbs pulled the covers up around her throat. Gibbs asked, "What do you want?"

"What I really want is to put a bullet in that head of yours," Creed snarled. "But I'll settle for you telling me where Miles is."

"What do you mean?"

"Don't give me that. You had your men let the buffalo out last night. In the end, it was a trap so Banks could kill me, but it didn't work."

Gibbs remained stoic.

"Now I want to know where Miles is."

Gibbs said nothing, just stared at the two men stubbornly.

Creed looked at the whore. "I'd move if I were you. Wouldn't want to get blood on that pretty face of yours."

Linc lifted the coach gun and aimed it at Gibbs.

"Wait!" Gibbs blurted. "I'm sure we can come to an arrangement."

"Start talking, Gibbs."

"He left. He's gone. Caught a train early this morning."

"Where to?"

"Chicago. Just up and left."

"What about Banks? Did he go too?"

"He wasn't going anywhere," Gibbs said.

"Why?"

"That buffalo made a mess of him. Broken arm and leg. Ribs, jaw. He's busted up inside. The doctor said it's only a matter of time before he dies. I'm surprised he's lasted this long. Then there are his burns."

"Where is he?" Creed asked.

"He's here in the club."

"Get up and take me to him," the Texan ordered.

Gibbs climbed out of bed and got dressed, then went down the hall with the two Faraday agents following him. When they reached the head of the stairs, two of his men were coming up the other way. Gibbs waved them down, not waiting for Creed or Linc to warn them off. When they reached the third-floor landing, Gibbs took them along the hallway to room 304.

"He's in there," he told them, indicating the door and stepping back to let them enter.

Creed opened the door. The room was dark since the drapes were drawn across the window. He cautiously walked inside with his gun at the ready.

Linc entered behind him, leaving Gibbs in the hallway. They could make out the lump on the bed with the covers pulled up, but that was it. Creed pointed at the window. "Let some light in, Linc."

Linc lowered his shotgun, walked over to the window, pulled back the drapes, and let light flood into the room. Creed winced when he got an initial look at the figure in the bed. The face was black and blue, so swollen it appeared as though the skin would split. The jaw was crooked and out of place since it had been broken. Creed said, "I guess the doctor didn't worry about fixing it because he was going to die."

"He don't look much, do he?" Linc observed. "Somehow, I thought he'd be bigger."

Creed frowned. "How big do you figure he is?"

Linc shrugged. "I don't know. It's hard to tell with him laying down and all. About as tall as you, I guess."

"That's what I figured. Now, I know that Banks is considerably *shorter* than me."

"Are you saying he isn't Banks? With a face like that, I bet his mother couldn't even recognize him."

An audible grunt came from out in the hall, followed by a thud. Creed turned his head and called, "You having trouble staying on your feet, Gibbs?"

His words were meant by silence.

"You hear me, Gibbs?"

Still nothing.

Creed stepped away from the bed and approached the doorway. When he reached it, he could see why Gibbs hadn't responded. He was dead, eyes wide and a gaping slash across his throat. "Son of a bitch."

Linc said, "I guess that answers our question."

The Texan looked down the hall and found it clear. "We need to get out of here before—"

"Hey! What are you do—"

It was Craig, Gibbs' bodyguard.

"Too late, I figure," Linc said as the man drew his weapon to fire.

The shotgun roared in the confined space, and the buckshot blasted down the hall and punched into the man's torso. He was thrown back by the velocity of the pellets and crashed to the floor.

"Damn it," Creed growled. "Come on."

He started down the hallway, stepping over the fallen man, and made it to the head of the stairs before looking down to see four more men coming up. *So much for six men*, Creed thought. "Go back, Linc," he snapped.

"Where to?" Linc asked. "We're cornered."

Creed looked back along the hallway. "Into the room."

"Which one?"

"Take your pick."

Linc kicked his way through a closed door and almost knocked it off its hinges. It crashed back against the wall, and the two men hurried inside. Fortunately, the room was empty. They went across to the window and looked out. Creed saw a ledge running along the front of the building, opened the window, and started to climb out.

"What the hell are you doing?"

"You want to stay in here?"

"Not really."

Once outside, they stood up, their backs pressed hard against the exterior wall and the toes of their boots hanging over the abyss. "This is a bad idea," Linc said.

"I know," Creed replied. "Follow me."

He edged along the building's façade until they reached the corner, and Creed looked around it. There was no more ledge. Tt stopped here.

"What now?" Linc asked. "We jump?"

"Not quite."

"Well, you'd better hurry because those *hombres* will work out where we are right smartly."

He watched as Creed reached around the corner of the building and disappeared. For a moment Linc panicked, but then he realized Creed was hanging in mid-air. He started lowering himself to the street.

When he reached the corner, Linc saw what Creed was doing; he was making his way down a drainpipe. "That'll work."

Linc began to follow him down, hoping the corner of the building would shield them from view.

Creed heard voices but couldn't see where they came from. He kept lowering himself until his boots touched the alley, then stepped smartly away from the pipe and waited for Linc, who'd somehow managed to both lower himself and retain his hold on the coach gun.

"That was interesting," he said to Creed, breathing hard from the exertion of the descent.

"Let's go. I've got a man to beat the hell out of."

* * *

The first body was at the top of the stairs. He'd been shot in the chest and had slumped onto the cold hard floor. The next one was just inside the door, his chest torn to shreds from a charge of buckshot. On the foyer stairs lay another man, who'd also been shot. He was still alive, but only just. His lifeblood dribbled down the stairs as it drained from his body. Another lay in front of the study door. He'd managed to get his weapon out before he died.

The bloody path was easily followed toward the action occurring inside the study where three men were.

O'Halloran sat on a chair, bleeding from a bullet wound in his leg. He ground his teeth together as pain radiated up to his brain. His eyes blazed. "Damn you."

"No, damn *you*," Creed said. "I don't know how or why, and quite frankly, I don't give a damn. Banks just killed Gibbs, and you had a hand in it. Killed your partner in crime. Wasn't what he gave you enough?"

O'Halloran smiled. "So, he did it. Quite frankly, I didn't know if he would."

"Where is Banks now?"

"I don't know. He's gone."

"Gone where?" demanded Creed.

"I told you, I don't know."

Linc shook his head in disgust. "We should just shoot the son of a bitch and be done with it, John."

"Nothing I'd like more," Creed allowed, "but there's been enough killing. Understand this, O'Halloran. We'll be back in a couple of weeks. If you're still here, we'll find you and finish what we started. Understood?"

The Irishman nodded. "Sure, sure."

Creed looked at Linc. "You happy with tha—"

The shotgun in Linc's hands came up and across before the remaining barrel exploded. O'Halloran flipped back with his chair, his chest torn to ribbons. His arms shot out, and his right hand opened. A small hideout gun skittered across the floor.

"Forgot about checking him for one of those, didn't you?" Linc said after the sound of the shot died.

Creed looked him straight in the eye and said, "No. I didn't."

* * *

"I'm going to cancel the show," McCoy said to Creed.

"Why?"

"After everything that happened, it just doesn't seem right."

"That's exactly why it should go on," Creed said. "You've still got an hour before it has to start. I'll have Hawk gather the cowboys, and they'll get it done."

"What if they try something else?"

"They won't," Creed told him. "Gibbs is dead, and Miles has left St. Louis for Chicago. Banks has disappeared again."

McCoy nodded. "All right, we'll do it. Tell Hawk to prepare the men."

Creed went and found Hawk. "It's still on. Get them ready. What are the buffalo like?"

"They're still on edge, but they always are."

"All right. Get it done."

"John?"

Creed saw Briar French approaching him. "What's up, Briar?"

"I'm coming with you to Chicago."

"How's the arm?"

"Damn thing is fine," he growled.

"Are you sure, Briar?"

French nodded. "Of course, I'm sure."

"Fine, then you're in."

"Thank God for that. I thought I was going to have to fight you."

Creed smiled. "Can't have that, can we?"

French shook his head. "Hate to make you look bad in front of the lady."

Creed frowned. French nodded over his shoulder, and the Texan turned to see Liza standing behind him. "Hello," she said.

"I'll leave you to it," French told him with a grin. "That was all I wanted."

"You look tired," Liza said to Creed.

"Now that you mention it, I kinda feel that way."

"Come on, I'll buy you a meal."

He smiled wanly. "I could use something to eat,"

he replied. "Do you have somewhere in mind?"

"It'll have to be close. The show goes on soon."

He nodded. "Lead the way."

They found a café where the food was simple but good and hot on a side street. From there, they went back to the stockyards and arrived just in time to watch the show.

At first, the cowboys opened the gates so the mustangs could buck and gallop around the pen. With lassos whirling and flying through the air, the cowboys roped the wild horses and allowed them to fight the lariats because it looked impressive, then finally brought the animals under control and led them out of the enclosure.

They repeated that with the two elk. The experienced ropers didn't have trouble with any of it, but the small crowd that had gathered cheered them anyway.

However, it was the buffalo they'd come to see, especially after word had gotten around about the escape of the ferocious beasts and the trail of destruction they had caused.

When the two shaggy creatures were let into the large yard, the crowd went quiet. They walked around the yard, letting out low grunts and pawing the dirt.

Then McCoy appeared, shouting to the crowd as he told them about the beasts before them. He introduced the three cowboys who would rope the animals, one of them being Hawk.

Creed and Liza watched as they worked the first buffalo before attempting to rope it. The big animal ran around the yard, doubling back every so often.

It tried to attack one of the mounted cowboys, so Hawk moved in and dropped a lasso over its horns, then leaned back on his horse and waited for the buffalo to take up the strain. When it did, the horse shuddered under the impact of the rope snapping taut. His mount leaned back as the rope tightened, but it lacked the power of the buffalo and couldn't hope to hold it.

Another cowboy moved in and dropped his rope over the animal's horns. The crowd cheered as his horse too took up the slack. Then came the third rider. He followed in the steps of the first two riders and did the same, and then it was over; the show was done. Nothing spectacular, just a simple but dangerous exhibition. Good practice for the Chicago show.

After they finished, McCoy came over, his face lit up a young child's. "It worked. By golly, it worked."

Creed nodded. "It did."

"We'll stay a couple of days so I can do business with some people, and then we leave for Chicago. I'd say all of you could do with some rest."

Chapter 18

Matthew Faraday reached under his suit jacket and touched the handle of the revolver. It was comforting to know it was there for the meeting he was about to have with the senator.

He'd sent a message to Wesley asking if they could get together and received an invitation to supper at the Roxbury Restaurant on Old Lexington Street. Word had reached him about the trouble with the buffalo and the death of Chad Rydell.

Creed had also told him about the death of Barney Gibbs and the Irishman O'Halloran. This case they were working was going to take some cleaning up, and a word in the right ear would go a long way. Until then, he had to deal with the issue of Senator Kurt Wesley.

"Does sir have a res...oh, good evening, Mr. Faraday," the maître d' greeted him. "Will you be dining at your usual table this evening?"

"No, thank you, Alex. I am dining with Senator Wesley tonight."

The maître d' named Alex nodded. "I see, sir." The man's voice had turned cold.

"Is there something wrong?"

"Uh, no, sir."

"Come on, Alex, I've been coming here long enough to know when you're holding something back."

"I'm sorry, sir, but…"

"Out with it."

Alex sighed. "I've heard stories around the capitol about the senator, sir."

"Good or bad?"

"Let's just say that I'd be wary of him, sir."

"Thanks, Alex."

"Very good, sir. I'll show you to the table."

Faraday followed in Alex's wake as he passed through numerous tables full of patrons and came to a stop at one by a window that overlooked a park across the street. Wesley wasn't a big man—thin, gray-haired, hawkish nose. Faraday knew him to be in his fifties.

The senator looked up and smiled mirthlessly. "Mr. Faraday, I presume?"

Faraday nodded. "Senator."

As Faraday sat down, Alex gave him a quick glance, then left. Wesley said, "I've heard a lot about you, Faraday. Word gets around Washington like a California wildfire."

"I've heard a lot about you too, Senator."

"Oh?"

Faraday left it at that, instead choosing to say, "Shall we order?"

"Let's. I hate talking business on an empty

stomach. It tends to turn a man off his food."

Faraday gave the room a cursory glance, and his practiced eye picked out two men he was sure were attached to Wesley. One was a big, broad-shouldered man; the other had a thin, stick-like frame. Opposites, but probably equally dangerous.

Faraday ordered steak with a sauce he'd never heard of. It was new to the menu, and he guessed there was a new chef in the kitchen. The steak came with potatoes and vegetables.

Wesley ordered something foreign to Faraday. When Wesley saw the expression on his face, he said, "New cook. He's French."

Faraday nodded as though that explained everything.

When their meals came, they ate in silence, the agency owner making sure to keep an eye on the senator's two men. Once they were finished eating, Wesley leaned back in his chair. "Shall we get to the bottom of why we're here, Faraday? Quite frankly, I've had better conversations dining alone."

Faraday nodded. "All right. Let's start with your business dealings with Hank Miles."

"Who?"

"Hank Miles. You know him. He's the one driving your business dealings out west."

Wesley's face remained blank. "I've no idea what you're talking about."

"No? I think you do. You're friends with Miles, and with the governor of Kansas, for that matter. But let's stick with Miles. You see, we were hired to protect the interests of the Hannibal and St. Joseph

Railroad. Miles has been trying to put Joe McCoy out of business in Abilene by any means necessary. He went as far as hiring an assassin named Banks. Killed a cattle buyer I knew personally. At first, we thought it was Miles on his own, but after putting a few things together, we realized there was no way in hell he could afford it. That's where you come in."

"I do declare, Faraday, you have a fanciful imagination," Wesley said.

"No, I don't think so. You see, when he got caught with the herd he stole, he sent word to you. You sent word to the governor, he became involved, and it all went away."

"I hope you have proof of these baseless accusations, Faraday," the senator growled, losing patience.

"Not yet, but we'll get it."

"Then I suggest you keep your lip buttoned. Washington can be a dangerous place for those who don't."

"I've no doubt about that, Senator, but I won't be bullied by you or anyone else. It's only a matter of time before I have what I need and your whole world comes falling down around your ears."

Faraday dropped his napkin on the table and stood up. Wesley glared at him and gave him a parting shot. "Pull your head in, Faraday. This is Washington, not some squalid frontier town you're in now. One snap of my fingers and I can break you."

"Snap away, Senator," Faraday said. "And by the way, you wouldn't last five minutes in one of those squalid frontier towns."

Wesley's face hardened as he watched Faraday

walk out. Once the agency man was gone, he signaled to his two men at the nearby table.

* * *

Faraday was sure he was being followed. As he made his way along the sidewalk, he could sense their presence rather than see whoever it was. After turning the corner, he stopped, then peered back around the building and saw the shadows shifting. There were two of them.

Faraday reached under his jacket and took out his revolver, then moved on. This time he kept to the shadows until he reached the next cross street, then walked to the other side. Behind him, a horsecar made its way along the street, passing beneath the sparse streetlamps.

Faraday could hear their footsteps now. The heels of the pursuers' shoes echoed from the hard surfaces of the buildings' walls.

He sped up, which forced them to do the same. When he came to an alley, he ducked in.

Faraday heard the footsteps coming quicker and more frantically. As he stood in the shadows and waited, a voice said, "Looks like you were right."

Beside the agency owner stood a big man who carried a Winchester rifle. He was part of Faraday's personal protection for the evening. "Is Lassiter in position, Ross?"

"Yes, sir." The agent noticed something odd about his boss. "Are you all right, sir?"

"We're about to declare war on a rich and powerful

man, Ross."

"The way I see it, sir, he's already done that. All we're going to do is bring him a little farther out of his hole."

As soon as his pursuers turned the corner, Faraday could see who they were—the two men he had seen at the table in the restaurant. Stunned by the sight of the two agency men, they desperately tried for their weapons.

The Winchester Ross held barked once, and a .44-caliber bullet exploded from the barrel. It punched into the chest of the larger man with the force of a mule's kick, and he staggered several steps before he collapsed.

From across the street, Lassiter fired. His bullet found the thin man, hitting him in the spine and dropping him on the spot. Ross stepped forward to check the bodies and found that both of the would-be killers were dead.

"You get out of here, sir," Ross said as Lassiter appeared from across the street. "We'll take care of these carcasses."

Faraday nodded. "All right. I might go and see our friend."

"You really want to go back there?"

"I want him to go to Chicago so we can connect him to Miles for certain."

"Keep an eye out then." Ross nodded at the dead men. "That fella plays dirty even for a politician."

* * *

It didn't take long for Faraday to reach the Roxbury. Alex saw him and frowned. "Did you forget something, Mr. Faraday?"

He shook his head. "No. Not really. Is the senator still here?"

"Yes, sir."

"Thanks. I'll find my own way."

He wove between the tables, retracing his footsteps from earlier to where Wesley was still seated, nursing a drink. When the senator looked up, he lost all the color in his face before gathering himself. He asked the same question Alex had.

"Did you forget something, Faraday?"

The agency owner shook his head. "No. But the next time you send men after me, you might want to make sure they're more capable than those two. Except I won't be around for a while. I'm headed out to Chicago to have a talk with your friend Miles. Once he sees how bad things are falling apart, there's no telling what he might say to try to save himself."

Before Wesley could speak, Faraday turned on his heel and walked out.

* * *

"Did you have any problems?" Faraday asked his men when they finally arrived at the office.

Ross shook his head. "No, boss."

"What did you do with them?" the agency owner asked as he poured his men a drink from the decanter.

Lassiter said, "Dropped them in the Potomac. How did your discussion go?"

"I told him I was heading to Chicago to talk to Miles."

"You think that'll get him there?"

Faraday shrugged. "I don't know, but it's worth a shot."

"What do you want us to do?" Ross asked.

"Go and get some sleep. Tomorrow, we're catching a train for Chicago. Be here by nine."

"Yes, sir."

The two men left the office, and Faraday sat there alone. He knew he'd only get one shot at wrapping up this case to his satisfaction. If Wesley went to Chicago, one of two things would happen: he and Miles would cease all their activities, or he'd have Miles killed so the link between them would be broken. Or...

Faraday thought for a moment. A third possibility he hadn't considered was that they would come after him and his men.

Faraday sighed and downed the last of his drink, then got to his feet, extinguished the lamps, and headed out of the office.

It wasn't until he hit the sidewalk that he realized something was wrong, and by then, it was too late. While it sank in, Faraday was falling, a loud ringing in his ears. He lay there, head spinning. Not long after, everything went dark, and Faraday lost consciousness.

As he was fading, he heard a voice say, "Now we'll see who does what, you son of a bitch."

* * *

252

When the two agency men returned to the office the following morning, there was no sign of Faraday. Ross scratched his head and said, "I don't like it. He's always here when he says he will be."

Lassiter grunted. "And the office was locked. Let's check his home."

They locked up and went back out. It was Lassiter who noticed the blood on the sidewalk. "Ross, look."

It wasn't a large patch, but there was too much for it to be good. "What do you think?"

"What I'm thinking is all bad."

"Me, too. We'd better send word to Creed that something is happening and then try to figure out what."

* * *

Faraday had an ache inside his head as big as Texas, and it was getting worse. It came in waves, and at its peak, his vision blurred, and it seemed like his head would explode. The scent of straw and manure filled his nostrils. From outside of wherever he was trussed up came voices. He tried to call out, but the gag was too well fixed, and all that escaped was a muffled grunt.

More voices sounded, then a crash. He was rocked violently and realized where he was—in an enclosed stock car that had just been hitched to a locomotive, presumably with others.

The door slid open with a screech, and a man appeared. He climbed in, followed by a second. They closed the door behind them and turned to where Faraday lay. One of them looked down at him and said, "The senator sends his regards, and he hopes you like train rides, detective man. It's going to be your last."

Faraday tried to speak, but again, all that escaped was a grunt. The man who had spoken leaned down and pulled the gag away. He asked, "What did you say?"

The agency owner swallowed to wet his throat, then rasped, "I'm guessing you don't know."

The sunlight filtering through the boards shone on the man's face as he frowned. "Know what?"

"That you're a dead man. They'll find you and kill you. Your boss just made this personal."

The man drew back a boot and kicked Faraday savagely in the ribs. The agency owner grunted as air rushed from his lungs, and he retched violently at the same time. He tried to draw in gulps of air, but at first, nothing happened. Then little by little, the ability to breathe came back to him.

The thug sneered. "You got something else to say, old man?"

"Give me a minute, and I'll think of something."

"Tough guy, huh?" the man said and drew his leg back to unleash another kick.

"Hold it," the other thug said. "Leave him. The boss wants him in one piece when we arrive."

"Where are we going?" Faraday asked.

"You'll find out," the first man growled before leaning down and replacing the gag. "Just because we have to keep an eye on you, it don't mean we have to listen to your yap."

Once again, the stock car lurched and started to move, only this time, it didn't stop as the locomotive at the head of the train rolled away from the railyard.

* * *

Creed screwed the telegram into a tight ball and squeezed it in the palm of his hand. Liza frowned at his expression and asked, "Is everything okay?"

He glanced at her, then shifted his gaze to Briar French and Linc Peters. "Faraday has disappeared."

"What happened?" French asked.

"I'm not sure."

"Do we need to go to Washington?" Linc inquired.

Creed shook his head. "No. Ross and Lassiter have it under control, or so they say. They were just letting me know."

"You figure it was Wesley, John?" Linc asked.

"Could be. I don't know. If I had to put money on it, I would say yes. Hopefully, they'll find Faraday before anything happens to him."

Creed took his drink from the table, threw it back, and replaced his glass on the polished surface. He ran his finger around the rim and stared at the emptiness. Like him, the others remained silent as they contemplated the news they had received.

It was Hawk who broke that silence when he appeared to give them news about preparations for the following day. "The buffalo are all fed and watered for the train ride tomorrow. So are the elk and the horses."

Linc shook his head. "I still can't believe you

actually got elk for the show."

Creed chuckled. "You should have seen his face when I told him Joe wanted them."

"Couldn't have been as bad as when he heard about the buffalo," French said.

"It was worse," Liza said with a grin.

"That's Faraday's fault," Hawk growled. "He was the one who suggested it."

"It was a wonderful idea," Creed said jovially.

"Easy to see you weren't the one who had to round them up."

"You said everything is good for tomorrow?" Creed prompted.

Hawk nodded. "Yeah. Lance and Ernie said the engine will be ready to leave at nine."

"All right, we'll be there."

"Are you dining with us tonight?" Liza asked Hawk.

He glanced at Creed apprehensively. The Texan said, "Join us. You can pay the bill."

"Great. That would be the only reason you'd want me around while you two are holding hands."

"No, I'll buy."

"In that case, I'll be there."

"Good," said Liza. "The rest of you should join us, too."

"Why not?" French said. "Seeing as Creed is buying."

"Great," the Texan moaned. "By the time we leave, I'll be broke."

Chapter 19

Two men struggled with a large trunk that went into the baggage carriage. Creed watched them battle to get the heavy item loaded and offered to give them a hand. "We're fine, sir," one of them answered.

Creed nodded. "Is there much left to be loaded?"

"No, sir. Once it's done, you'll be ready to leave."

The Texan grunted. They had intended to be gone by now, but some mechanical holdup had delayed them for an hour. They'd be lucky to get into Chicago before dark.

While they waited, McCoy'd had some of the hands work on the presentation of the cars, adding more streamers and a touch of paint. Hawk gave the buffalo and the other animals extra feed and some water to tide them over.

"Are we done, John?" McCoy asked.

"Almost."

"Any word about Faraday?"

Creed shook his head. "None."

"Damn it, this is all my fault. If—"

"No, it's not," the Texan stated. "All you're trying to do is make something happen. You just concentrate on that. Let us worry about the rest."

McCoy's solemn expression lifted. "I managed to talk a couple of buyers into coming to Abilene. They'll be there when we get back. Hopefully, they'll have more competition when we return."

"Looks like Bernie Warriner will be able to sell his herd, then."

McCoy nodded eagerly. "I sent him a wire to let him know."

"We're ready to go," Lance, the engineer, interrupted.

Creed looked at him. "Then there's no point in standing around anymore. Let's see what the Windy City has to offer."

* * *

The landscape slid past with every turn of the locomotive's wheels. Creed sat talking to Liza for a while, then they both dozed for a time. It wasn't until Linc shook him awake that he was aware something was wrong. He opened his eyes and said, "What is it?"

"Come with me."

Creed got to his feet, trying not to disturb the still-sleeping Liza. The two men walked to the rear of the car and stopped. Linc's face grew serious. "We can't find Hawk."

"What do you mean?"

"It's like he's vanished from the train. He's not on it."

"Damn it," Creed growled. "When was the last time someone saw him?"

Linc shrugged. "An hour, as far as I can figure."

"There's not that many places he could be. Check again. Also, send one of the hands over the top and get Lance to stop the train."

"All right. Are you going to tell Liza?"

Creed shook his head. "Not yet."

Ten minutes later, the train slowed to a stop. Creed stepped down and moved to the locomotive, where he found Lance perplexed at the order to do so. "What the hell is going on, John? Why was we ordered to stop?"

"Hawk's missing."

"Missing?"

"That's what I said."

"How could a man go missing on a damn train?" Ernie asked.

"I don't know."

"How long are we going to be stuck here?"

"Until I tell you to move," Creed replied.

"All right. We'll just sit up here and wait for you."

Creed looked back along the train and saw Linc motioning to him. He started back and had about reached him when Liza climbed down in front of him. "What's going on, John?" she asked.

"We have a problem. I'll be with you in a minute."

"What kind of problem?"

He looked at Linc and then back at her. He sighed. "Hawk is missing."

Alarm appeared on her face. "What do you mean, missing? He was on the train. How could he go missing on the train?"

He touched her arm, but she shrugged it off. He tried again, but she stepped back. "Answer me, John."

"I don't know, Liza. Wait here, I have to go see Linc."

He could see by her face that she wanted to ask more questions, but she didn't. He turned away and walked over to Linc. "What is it?"

"Follow me."

Linc took him to where the baggage car was coupled with the first stock car. He pointed at the coupling. "You see it?"

"Looks like blood."

"That's what I figured," he agreed.

"You thinking he fell off the train?" Creed asked.

"Looks that way," Linc said. "I'm not sure, though. Why would he be out here?"

"Checking on the animals?"

"Maybe?"

Creed bent and touched the coupling. The blood was still tacky. "This didn't happen that long ago. If it had been longer, the passage of the train would have dried it out. Makes a difference between a couple of miles and twenty."

"That's something, I guess."

"Have someone get my horse off the train. I'm going back to have a look."

"I'm coming with you," Linc told him.

"Fine, have one saddled for you too."

Linc hurried away and Creed looked at Liza, who was still watching him. "Damn it," he muttered.

He walked over to her and stopped. "What is it?"

she asked.

"We think he might have fallen off the train. Linc and I are going to ride back to see if we can find him."

"But he could be miles back along the track."

"We think he's not too far. We found some blood, and it was still wet. If it had been there for twenty miles or so, it would be dry."

"Let me come with you?" Liza said.

"No, stay here. We won't be gone long."

"John—"

"Not this time, Liza."

Her head bowed, and her shoulders started to quake as silent sobs wracked her body. He took her in his arms. "We'll find him, Liza. I promise."

She looked up at him with tears in her eyes. "I know, John. But will he be alive when you do?"

* * *

Creed and Linc rode away from the train ten minutes later, following the iron rails as they cut southwest. After an hour of riding, the sun was starting its downward track toward the western horizon, and the heat of the day was starting to cool.

"Can't be much further," Linc said to Creed as they rode through a dry creek bed and up the other bank.

"You'd think not," he replied.

Another mile slid by, then Creed noticed crows circling in the distance, black specks against the blue backdrop. "You see them?" he asked Linc.

"Yeah. I got them."

They spurred their mounts, and the animals broke

into a lope. The distance between the riders and their destination shrank quickly and an inanimate lump became visible in the grass beside the tracks.

Creed reined in the buckskin, and Linc did the same with his horse. They dismounted and walked slowly toward the figure. The cawing of the crows grew in intensity as they became angry with the intruders. Creed looked down at the form at his feet. There was no mistaking who it was.

Hawk's eyes were wide in death. There was blood on the side of his head, and the Texan guessed the wound had occurred when he'd hit it. Then he noticed the blood on Hawk's shirt collar in the back and a puzzled expression came over his face.

Creed got down on his knees and looked closer.

"What's wrong?" Linc asked.

"I'm not sure."

He looked closer still, then he saw it—the puncture wound on the back of the neck. "Damn it."

"What?"

"Our old friend Banks is back."

"What do you mean back?"

"He killed the buyer Faraday sent out the same way."

"I'm not doubting you, John, but how does Banks kill Hawk on the train when there is nowhere to hide? Me and the others went through the damned thing looking for Hawk. If he was there, we would have found him."

"I don't know, Linc, but he managed it somehow."

"He has got to still be there, then," Linc offered.

"It's possible."

"We have to get back."

Creed nodded slowly. "After we take care of Hawk. We'll get some rocks and cover him up."

"You sure? I could do this if you want and come after you later."

"The others are there. I don't think Banks will come out of hiding to do anything when all of the others are on hand."

"You're probably right."

Creed nodded. He hoped he was.

* * *

It was after dark when they arrived back at the stopped train. Liza sought Creed out as soon as she heard he had returned. "I'm sorry, Liza. He didn't make it."

"What happened?" she asked through tears.

"He was murdered."

McCoy growled in anger and frustration. "This is out of control. Death has dogged us ever since I came up with this blasted idea. I might as well give up to save more lives."

"Don't you dare," Liza said. "This has come too far for it to end like this."

"She's right, Joe," Creed agreed. He turned to Linc. "Search the train. We don't move from here until we find him."

"You might want to hope another train don't come along," Lance said, overhearing the conversation.

Creed hadn't thought about that. He'd been too caught up with what he'd been doing. "When do you figure that might happen?"

"Only God and the railroad can answer that."

"Then we'd better hurry."

They searched the train thoroughly—every car inside and out—and came up empty. Nothing.

Briar French said, "If he was here, John, he's gone. I still can't work out how he got on in the first place."

Creed called to the engineer. "Lance, how far are we from Chicago?"

"Couple of hours."

"Is there anywhere close to here that a man could go for transport?"

"No. Not that I know of."

French said, "He must have hidden somewhere we'd least expect it."

Creed stared at him through the darkness, which was now illuminated by the glow of a half-moon. "What are you thinking?" French asked.

"Get a lantern and come down to the baggage car."

A few minutes later, French and Linc joined Creed at the car. Creed opened the door and went inside. The interior was illuminated by the lantern's orange glow. Creed looked around, his eyes searching everything stacked inside.

"What are you looking for, John?" Linc asked.

Creed held up his left hand for silence while he drew the Colt with his right. He then pointed at the large trunk the two men had loaded back in St. Louis and signaled for Linc to open the lid.

Both of them moved forward, and the Colt in Creed's fist pointed at the trunk. Linc reached out but stopped and pointed at the latch, which was undone. The hammer went back on the Texan's six-gun with a loud click. Linc waited for a moment, then Creed nodded.

Linc heaved the lid open as fast as he could. It fell back, and the light from the lantern illuminated the empty trunk.

Creed muttered a curse and let the hammer down on the Colt. He holstered it and lashed out with his boot, which hit the side of the trunk, causing it to move a few inches. "I saw two men load this on back in St. Louis, and they struggled to lift it. I even offered to give them a hand."

"You couldn't have known, John," French told him.

"Makes me wonder if the ones who loaded it knew."

"Well, he's long gone now."

Creed looked out at the darkened landscape. "Let's get out of here."

* * *

It was the dog that gave away the approach of the stranger. The mutt stood under the awning of the small farmhouse, barking at the night. Its owner opened the door and walked out behind it, holding a Henry rifle. "What is it, Rags?" he asked the dog. "Coyotes about tonight, huh?"

"Not unless you call me a coyote, sir," the man stated as he emerged into the light spilling into the yard from the door and window.

"Who are you, mister?" the man asked, wondering why the stranger talked kind of funny.

"I'm but a weary traveler set afoot by his horse's misfortune of finding a hole in the dark."

"You lost your horse?"

"Sadly, yes."

A woman's voice sounded from inside, out of sight of the doorway. "Who's there, Marty?"

"Stay inside, Josie," he called over his shoulder.

"You couldn't spare some water, mister?" the stranger asked.

The farmer studied the man in black and said, "There's a trough near the barn."

"Marty, invite him in. We've got some food left over from supper we can give him."

"No, Josie. We don't know him."

"He looks tired, Marty. What harm could he be? We can give him food and shelter. I'm sure he'd appreciate it."

"Yes, ma'am," the man said. "I sure would."

"Damn it, Josie."

"Go on, invite him in."

Marty looked at the stranger, uncertainty on his face. He shrugged. "All right, come ahead, mister. Just don't try anything funny. I'll keep this Henry right handy."

"Much obliged," Rudy Banks said and limped forward, his right hand behind his back with a thin-bladed knife tucked against his forearm.

"You hurt your leg?" Marty asked.

Banks stopped so the homesteader could see him clearly. Not only did he have a limp, but his face was also swollen on one side, and it was black and blue with a large bruise.

"You take a tumble, mister?"

Banks nodded. "Something like that."

* * *

"Are all of the animals unloaded?" Creed asked.

"Yeah," Linc told him.

The smell of the Chicago stockyards hung heavy in the air, and the lowing of cattle filtered through the darkness. Linc's nose wrinkled. "This place stinks."

Creed had to agree. So many odors in one place and he knew that once it rained, the smell would grow even worse. "At least the yards here will hold the buffalo," he said. "Let's go find McCoy."

They found him talking to one of the yard managers, making sure the animals would have plenty of fresh water and food. When he was done, he turned to the two Faraday men.

"I've arranged for all of us to stay at a hotel which isn't too far away."

Creed raised his eyebrows. "All of us? The cowboys too?"

"That's right."

"How?"

"Let's just say that with the publicity this will bring, the owner was more than happy to be part of it."

"What publicity?" Linc asked.

"I have an interview with a newspaperman tomorrow before the show the next day."

"Not tomorrow?"

McCoy shook his head. "No, I want word to get around more than it already has. The more buyers, the better."

"All right, this is your show. Mind you, the thought of a fancy hotel does sound inviting."

* * *

"If you say anything, I'm going to shoot you," Creed growled.

"I thought I heard someone say 'fancy hotel,'" Linc said with a wink at Liza. "Can't remember who it was, but he was obviously mistaken."

Liza giggled and grabbed Creed's arm. "I bet they have rats."

"God, I hope not."

A middle-aged man with unkempt hair came to the desk. He scowled at the three of them and said, "If I'd known you were going to be this late, I'd never have agreed to this."

"We're sorry," Liza said to placate the man. "It's been an awful time."

"Yeah, well, it ain't easy running a hotel."

"Is that what it is?" Linc whispered to Creed.

"What was that?" the man asked.

"I said it was a fine establishment."

The man eyed him suspiciously, and Liza couldn't hide her grin. When he glared at her, she said, "Could we have our rooms, please?"

The man grunted and mumbled under his breath, then grabbed three keys and tossed them on the countertop. Liza picked up two and left the other behind. "Do they have big beds?"

"They do, but—" his eyes widened. "Wait a minute, you only took two keys."

Liza grinned broadly. "I did, didn't I?"

With that, they started toward the stairs.

At the top of the stairs on the second floor, Liza gave

Linc his key. "Are you going to join us for breakfast?"

"I'm not sure," he replied, looking around at the wallpaper peeling off the walls.

"Not here, silly," she told him.

"In that case, I'd be happy to."

"Good. We'll see you then."

They went to their rooms. Once inside, Creed sat on the bed and fell backward, spreading his arms out. "I feel like I could sleep for a week."

"What's the bed like?" Liza asked.

"Like putting your bedroll on rocks."

"Wonderful. I might sleep on the floor then."

"Hmm?"

"I said, I might sleep on the floor."

"Okay."

"John, did you understand what I just said?"

"Yes."

"What did I say?"

"Hmm?"

"What did I say?"

"You were going to shut the door."

"Goodnight, John."

"Goodnight."

* * *

The door of the car slid open, and Faraday saw a shadow standing in the opening. The two men who were inside with him came to their feet and walked across. The figure said, "Bring him with you."

Faraday recognized the voice as Wesley's. "Where are we?"

"You'll find that out eventually."

The two men grabbed him and half-dragged, half-carried him to the door. They thrust him outside, and he fell to the hard-packed ground beside the rails. He grunted as air rushed from his lungs. Boots crunched on gravel as the two men jumped down beside him and roughly jerked him to his feet.

A gust of wind tugged at Faraday's coat, carrying with it a smell he recognized. They were in Chicago. That had to be the stockyards.

Wesley said, "Bring him. We'll take him to the house, and then we have to meet with Miles. I need to know what is happening."

"Senator," one of the men said, "why don't we just kill him and be done with it?"

"Because he's the highest card in our deck. We damn well need him."

"Yes, sir."

"Now, do as I told you."

* * *

There was a knock at the door, and Hank Miles was instantly alert. He placed his coffee cup on the table, stared at the door, and waited, filled with apprehension. It came again.

"Who is it?"

"It's me. Open the door."

The voice was different, but there was no mistaking who it was.

Miles opened the door and let Banks into the room. His face was still swollen, and the bruises were changing color. He limped across the floor and sat in a chair. He looked at Miles and asked, "What have I missed?"

"I know *who* you missed. Joe McCoy. What happened?"

"It couldn't be helped. I was found by the man they called Hawk and had to get rid of him. They were searching the train, so I had to jump."

"My partner, or should I say my financier, is coming to Chicago."

"Why is he coming here?"

"I don't know. Maybe because of what's been happening. It hasn't exactly been a success. McCoy is still alive, the herds of cattle that are coming up the trail are headed for Abilene, and it looks like the buyers might just head back to buy McCoy's cows. As it is, we...*he* stands to lose thousands."

"Do you want me to—"

"I want you to kill McCoy. I'll pay extra if you can get it done. All right?"

Banks nodded, then winced as pain shot through his neck.

"Are you up to it?" Miles asked.

"I'll do it," Banks said. Abruptly, he took out a handkerchief and dabbed the corner of his swollen eye with it. It was white with lace trim—a woman's handkerchief.

"You really do look like hell."

"You just worry about yourself and have my money ready."

Miles was about to respond when another knock sounded. Miles looked at Banks, who shrank to the rear of the room, taking his revolver out.

"Who is it?" Miles asked.

"It's me, you damned fool. Open the blasted door."

Relief flooded Miles as he strode toward the door. When he opened it, Wesley stood there with two other men.

"About damn time," the senator growled as he stepped into the room. The men with him entered but remained on guard near the door.

Wesley pointed at Banks. "Who is he?"

"That's Banks."

"Banks who, dammit?"

"Rudy Banks. The—"

"The killer?"

"Yes."

"Looks like he's not been making a good job of it," Wesley commented. "What happened to you, Banks?"

"Disagreement with a buffalo," Banks said.

"Are you one of the useless ones that Miles hired?"

The killer's good eye flared, then his lips peeled back in a lopsided grin. "I'm quite capable, Senator."

Wesley glared at Miles and then at Banks. "You know who I am?"

"I've heard of you in Washington circles. Never seen you until now. Can't say I'm much impressed."

"Stick around, son, and I'll give you something to be impressed about. Providing you're any good in that shape."

"I guess we'll find out."

"What did Miles hire you for anyway?"

"I hired him to kill that blasted buyer Matthew Faraday sent to Abilene," Miles interrupted.

"Yes, Abilene. Tell me everything, Miles. I want it all."

Miles took him through it from start to finish. Wesley listened to him in silence until he stopped.

"I'm not impressed, Miles," Wesley stated. "I invested a lot of money for cattle. All you've given me lately is trouble, and not only that, Matthew Faraday comes to me and threatens to upset everything."

"He what?"

"You heard me. Faraday came to me. He had pieced everything together—you, me, and our friend in Kansas. All you had to do was put McCoy out of business. Now, I had to come all the way out here and fix things myself."

"I'm sorry, Kurt," Miles apologized. "Once Faraday got involved, things got kind of complicated. I did manage to get that herd, though."

"Yes, with my help. I'm meant to be a silent partner in all this., but here I am, out of the darkness, front and center. I should have left you where I found you."

"You don't mean that, Kurt," Miles said tentatively. "We're almost there. Once Banks kills McCoy, it'll be done."

"Damn it, Miles, you still don't see. It should never have gotten this far."

"I agree, Kurt. But Faraday—"

Wesley looked at Banks and nodded slightly.

The killer started toward Miles. The man's eyes widened as he realized what was about to happen. "Wait! I can fix this."

"You already tried, Miles," Wesley said disinterestedly. "You've already tried."

* * *

They left the body where it lay. There was no need to hide it since the building couldn't be linked to Wesley. Once outside, they climbed into a buggy. The two bodyguards sat up front, and the senator and Banks sat in the back. Out of the blue, Wesley said, "I have Faraday."

"What do you plan to do with him?"

"Use him to make my problems go away."

"You'll have to kill him eventually," Banks said. "But I suppose you already know that."

Wesley stared at Banks as he took the handkerchief out and dabbed his eye. "Son, I bet that hurts like a bitch."

"Pain is what you make of it," Banks replied. "You let it get the best of you, or you embrace it."

"I take it that you do the latter?"

"It is an acquired taste."

Wesley nodded and said, "I want you to kill McCoy, and this is how we're going to do it."

Chapter 20

"Has there been any news about Faraday?" Creed asked Linc.

"Not a word."

Creed sipped his coffee and slipped into thought. After a minute or so, he said, "I hate this."

"Yeah, the coffee tastes like a horse stepped in it."

"Not the—"

"I know what you mean."

Creed looked around the café. They were waiting for French to return so they could work out a strategy for the following day and McCoy's big show. They could only guess that McCoy would still be a target, and Miles would try to stop the show any way he could. If not, it would be all over because as it stood, according to McCoy, he had lined up more than a handful of buyers to be present.

"Is this a private gathering, or can anybody join?"

The voice was different, but there was no mistaking it. Creed glanced at Banks, and it took all his willpower to not pull his Colt and put a bullet in his head. The killer could see the anger in the Texan's eyes and said, "Before you go and do something stupid, you might want to know we have your boss."

"Where?" Creed demanded, not willing to trust himself to say more.

Banks sat down in a third chair and dabbed his eye with the lace handkerchief.

"That buffalo messed you up some," Creed observed. "Shame it didn't kill you. Where is Faraday?"

"He's safe for now. Probably won't stay that way for long, though."

"What do you want?" Linc asked.

"You."

Linc frowned. "Me?"

"All of you. Creed, you, and that other one."

"Briar?" Creed asked.

"If that's his name."

"Why?" Creed asked.

Banks dabbed his eye again. "Because you are interfering in business that doesn't concern you."

"You want us out of the way so you can get at McCoy," Linc stated.

Creed nodded. "I agree. Not going to happen."

"Then your boss will die. It's simple," Banks said with a shrug.

The killer started to get to his feet.

"Wait," Creed said. "Where?"

"The lake docks. There is a warehouse with a sign saying Wright Shipping. In there."

"When?"

"Tonight, a couple of hours after dark. I will warn you, if you try to hide McCoy before you come, we will know about it."

Creed stared at the killer. "Fine. We'll be there."

"Don't get any ideas, John," Banks cautioned him. "If you try something, or all three of you aren't there, your boss will take a swim in Lake Michigan. Is that understood?"

"Yeah, we understand," Creed replied. "What about Miles? Will he be there?"

Banks dabbed his eye once more. "I'm afraid Mr. Miles recently became unemployed. He had a falling out with his boss."

"You mean, the senator ran out of patience with him," Linc supplied.

"Something like that. If that is all, I'll leave you now. By the way, don't be late."

They watched him limp away, then Linc said, "I'd like to put a slug in that son of a bitch right about now."

"Me, too," Creed agreed.

"You know that once we're out of the way, he's going to go after McCoy, don't you?"

"That's the part that worries me. It's out there for us to see. He made no attempt whatsoever to conceal it, and that means he's confident of getting it done."

"He should be," Linc pointed out. "The docks are miles away from the hotel."

"We'll just have to do our best."

Before Linc could say more, French appeared. "You two look a mite worried about something."

He sat down, and Creed and Linc told him about their meeting with Banks. "Well, that's interesting."

"That's it?" Linc said. "That's all you've got? No suggestions?"

"I can think of one," French said. "But you're not going to like it."

***

Creed put the Colt in Liza's hand and said, "Take it. Having two loaded weapons is better than one."

"What about you?"

"I have mine. That one was Hawk's. I took it off him before we buried him."

Liza stared at it for a moment before tucking it into her pants. "Thank you, John."

"Listen, I have no doubt you can do this, but it's up to you."

Liza nodded. "I hope that son of a bitch tries, John. I'd like to put a bullet in his damn hide."

She sounded positive, but her eyes told another story. He put a hand on her shoulder. "We'll try to get back as soon as possible."

"Don't rush. It'll give me more time to shoot pieces off Banks."

"You put a bullet in him for me, Liza," Linc said. "And a couple more for the others."

"I will, don't worry."

French joined them. "Time to go."

They looked at McCoy. "You all right, Joe?"

"I'm fine," he said, patting the six-gun on the small table. "Go get your boss back."

Creed leaned in and kissed Liza, then pulled back. "Make them count."

"Every last one of them."

* * *

The waterfront had its own fetid smell, which was hard to describe. All the garbage that had built up around the edge of the lake was rotting. Rats could be heard scurrying around it, their high-pitched screeches piercing the night. So could the growls and cries of the feral cats that searched for them to feed on.

Water lapped the piers, and the wind, which had been strong earlier in the day, had dropped to almost nothing.

Creed tightened his grip on his Yellow Boy and continued along the front of the warehouse, looking for anything that would indicate this was the building they were looking for. Then French pointed out the light in a window of one farther along. "I guess that's it," he said in a low voice.

"That would be my guess, too," Linc said, cradling his shotgun.

"Let's go have a look."

They reached the warehouse and found the large door at the front partially open. Creed peered in and saw a man standing about ten feet away holding a rifle. He turned to the others and said, "This is it."

They walked inside, taking the man by surprise. He swung his weapon around. Creed held up his hand and said, "Take it easy, friend, we're here to see the senator."

* * *

Liza didn't know what it was, but the hunch that told her something was wrong made her blood pump through her veins faster. She gripped the gun tightly in her hand and snicked the hammer back. She was hiding in the darkened bedroom of McCoy's suite, if that's what it could be classed as. McCoy, on the other hand, was in the main living area.

She crossed to the door and turned the knob. Once the latch was free, she opened it slightly to see what was happening on the other side. When she couldn't see anything, she swung it wider. McCoy was sitting on the sofa, a hard, lumpy seat that was about as comfortable as a bench in a stagecoach. He glanced at her. "What's wrong?"

Liza shook her head. "I don't know. I have this feeling I used to get on the trail from Texas that something is wrong. I can't explain it."

McCoy spread his hands out. "As you can see, it's all quiet."

"Yeah, too quiet."

She walked across to the door leading to the hallway. Turning the key slowly, she opened the wooden door wide enough to peer out. The dimly lit hall was clear, so Liza closed it and turned the key to secure it.

Liza shrugged. "Maybe I'm getting jumpy."

McCoy smiled at her as she walked past him. He reached out and took her hand. "Don't worry, Liza, you're doing a great job. Creed couldn't have done any better than choosing you to watch over me."

"We'll see."

Liza walked back into the darkened bedroom

and closed the door. She stood transfixed and breathed a sigh of relief as the cool breeze from the window washed over her, relaxing. She frowned. The window—

Everything went black.

* * *

"Well, here we are," Wesley said with more than a hint of glee in his expression.

Creed stared at the man, who was flanked by two heavyset bodyguards. "Where is he, Wesley?"

"He's close by," the senator assured him.

"So, what now?" Linc asked.

"We wait."

"For what?"

"Confirmation," Wesley replied.

"You mean confirmation that McCoy is dead, right?" Creed asked.

The senator nodded. "Something like that. I expect word within the hour, so make yourselves comfortable. Oh, and drop your weapons."

"Why would we do that?" asked French.

"Because if you don't, I will have your boss killed."

"For a senator, he ain't very smart, John. Wouldn't you say?" Linc chuckled.

Creed nodded. "Not very."

"Do you find something amusing?" Wesley demanded, his patience wearing thin.

"You could kill our boss," Creed theorized, "but then one of us will kill you."

"What makes you think you will succeed?"

"What makes you think we won't?"

Creed sensed rather than saw Linc stiffen beside him. His eyes darted around the gloomy interior until they caught the slight movement of a figure high atop a stack of crates. They tracked further along and found another. The senator had been playing for time so his ambush could move into place.

From the corner of his mouth, Linc said, "Creed."

"I see them."

Wesley said, "I'm still waiting for you to put your weapons down."

"Keep waiting," Creed snapped and shot the man on Wesley's right.

* * *

The voices seemed distant, but in time they came closer. Liza gave a soft moan as the pain in her head grew more intense. She raised her hand to the back of her head and winced as agony shot through it. The hand came away wet, and she started to recall where she was and what she was doing.

Liza rolled over and pushed herself onto her feet. The bedroom spun briefly before she steadied herself and took a lurching step toward the light filtering through the door. The voices grew louder as she drew closer to the opening. She peered through the gap and saw McCoy tied to a chair in the center of the room. In front of him with his back to her was a man she assumed was Banks. It had to be him.

Liza's hand dropped, searching for her gun. It wasn't there. She grasped futilely for the other, and her heart fell when she discovered it too was gone. Then she saw them on a small side table near where McCoy was seated.

"Wait! No!" she heard McCoy gasp and saw the small knife in the killer's hand as it slowly rose from his side.

Clenching her jaw, Liza burst through the doorway and threw herself at the killer.

Liza's body jarred as she crashed into him. Her loud scream wasn't about her being scared but to try to put the killer off-balance.

They spilled to the floor, and the knife skidded across the boards when Banks lost hold of it. The two of them thrashed around as Banks tried to dislodge her. Liza clawed his lopsided face with her stunted nails. Banks hissed as they dug into his cheek and pain burned through his disfigurement.

The killer struck out with a fist, and lights flashed through Liza's head. She tasted blood in her mouth, but she wasn't about to give up just yet. She'd had blows from unbroken horses that were harder than that.

"Try again," Liza said through gritted teeth and hit him with a closed fist.

Stunned, Banks desperately rolled away from her. Liza scrambled to her feet and spat blood on the floor. Strands of her hair hung down in her face, and her eyes rolled like a wild Texas mustang's.

With a high-pitched shout, Liza charged Banks. Her shoulder hit him as he was coming to his feet, the point of it striking just below his armpit with all the force she could put into it.

She knew she'd hurt him, perhaps even broken ribs; the sharp intake of breath and the pained grunt told her that. He lashed out wildly, startled that a woman could injure him.

The back of his hand caught Liza under the jaw and caused her to throw her head back. She reeled away, stunned by the hard blow, and fell onto her stomach. Liza desperately tried to regain her feet.

She was acutely aware of McCoy's urgent shouts and was almost to her hands and knees when Banks crashed onto her back. With a grunt, Liza was forced onto her stomach once more. Another blow hit her in the back of the skull, forcing her forehead to smack down the wooden floor.

Liza screamed more from frustration rather than pain. Adrenaline surged through her as she tried to dislodge the killer from her back. His hands wrapped around her throat and began to squeeze. Banks' face was near her ear. "I did not want to kill you, but you leave me no choice."

The force the killer was using increased, and Liza's right arm stretched out ahead of her as though she were reaching for a miracle. She could feel her air becoming more and more restricted. Her hand flailed around, and then her fingers touched it. They flicked across it at first but then came back and knocked it aside.

Liza's tear-filled eyes focused on the object—Banks' knife. She stretched her arm out for it, reaching...reaching. Her fingers fell painfully short. She grunted as she tried desperately to stretch the last few inches to the weapon.

Banks saw what she was doing and drove a fist into her outstretched arm, making it recoil from the knife. His hand quickly rejoined the other in his strangling grip on her throat.

Liza tried to scream in frustration, but her voice was a gagging sound choked off by the killer's grip. Her air was almost totally cut off, and Liza knew she was going to die despite her efforts.

In a final bid, her right hand sought the knife. This time, she fell even shorter than before. Somehow Banks had edged her backward, putting the weapon well out of reach.

Then something moved—a boot. Liza caught sight of it as it nudged the weapon's handle. The knife skidded forward, and Liza felt a surge of strength course through her rapidly tiring body.

Her right hand closed over the knife's handle, and her fingers locked it in. With a loud grunt, she brought the knife back past her ear and felt it stop suddenly. Something wet and warm splashed the side of her face, then the weight upon her back shifted violently and the steel band around her throat sprang open.

With most of the killer's weight gone, Liza rolled away and scrambled back until she was well out of reach. She stopped and stared at Banks, who was grasping his throat, from which the knife protruded.

A steady stream of blood ran briskly between the killer's fingers and his mouth worked like that of a fish out of water. His expression was panicked and puzzled. Banks' desperate motions slowed as his life drained out of him until eventually, he was still.

Still working at getting air into her lungs, Liza refused to move in case the killer climbed to his feet. McCoy asked, "Are you all right?"

She glanced at him then back to the corpse of Banks, unwilling to take her eyes off him yet. She nodded shakily. "I...I think so."

"Is he dead?"

"I hope so. I don't fancy going through all that again."

* * *

The man Creed had shot dropped like a stone with a .44 Henry slug in his head. The other man beside Wesley grabbed for his weapon but never cleared leather. Linc's shotgun crashed, and the thug was slammed back with a chest full of buckshot.

Figures emerged from the darkness and opened fire. The air filled with lead, and Creed felt the heat of a passing bullet. Briar French opened up with his six-gun, shooting a man who stood atop one of the crate stacks.

The man let out a cry and tumbled forward, landing with a sickening thud on the hard floor of the warehouse.

The rest of the gunfight was messy—men standing tall, shooting wildly at figures without aiming properly. Bullets flew chaotically, ricocheting off the floor and the walls. Linc cried out in pain, and Creed glanced to his right. The agent was down on one knee, jaw clenched against the pain of his leg wound.

286

Two more of Wesley's shooters fell, wounded, one gut shot, while the second took a slug from French in his chest. Linc called to Creed, "Find Faraday!"

The Texan nodded and worked his way to the right, firing the last few rounds from his Yellow Boy as he went. He dropped the empty carbine on the floor and pulled his Colt. Behind him, the gunfire ceased. He circled around a tall stack of crates and saw Faraday tied to a chair in a large open space. Standing next to him were two men. One was Wesley, and the other was perhaps the only gunman the senator had left.

Creed stepped into the open and called, "Hey!"

The gunman whirled, and Creed shot him. The slug punched into his chest and spun him before he fell face-down. The Texan shifted his aim so the smoking barrel of the Colt was centered on the senator's chest.

"How do you want to do this, Senator?" Creed asked as he walked toward them.

Wesley's hand dove under his coat and emerged with a small hideout gun. The Colt in Creed's fist roared again and the senator dropped his weapon, clutching his bloody arm. His face wrinkled into a mask of anger and pain.

"Damn you!" Wesley rasped. He swayed a couple of times and fainted dead away from the shock of being shot.

"You all right, Mr. Faraday?" Creed asked his boss.

"I'll live," Faraday growled. "But you shouldn't have come. It was all a ploy to get you away from McCoy."

"We know that," Creed allowed. "And right now, I have to get back to the hotel. The others will help you."

"What? Don't you leave me tied up here, John," Faraday called after him. "John, untie me. John? *John!*"

As he ran past Linc and French, he said, "The boss is back there. As you can hear, he's fine. I have to get back to Liza."

* * *

When Creed entered the room, the body remained in the position it had been in at the culmination of the fight, complete with protruding knife. He took one look at it and then glanced around the room.

She was standing near the window, looking at him. "Liza?"

When she hurried to him, he enveloped her in his arms. There were no tears, just a long period of silence. McCoy stepped forward and said, "I'd be dead if it weren't for her."

Creed nodded.

Liza stepped back and looked into his eyes. "I did it. He got what he deserved. The others?"

Creed nodded. "It's over."

* * *

Faraday slapped Creed on the back and said, "Well done, son. Assignment successful."

"A whole heap of folks deserve the credit for that," Creed replied. "I was just part of it."

Linc sat with his wounded and bandaged leg up

288

on a chair, resting it. Briar French was sipping a glass of brandy. Joe McCoy was still coming to terms with the fact that his buffalo train had been so fruitful. He had at least seven buyers going to Abilene on the next train, intending to buy all the cattle the Texans could supply.

Creed looked at Liza. Her bruises were evident, but instead of being embarrassed by them, she wore them as badges of pride. He smiled at her. "Are you ready?"

She nodded. "I'm ready when you are."

"Wait," said Faraday. "Where are you going?"

"I'm going with Liza to Texas," Creed explained. "Help her sort out a few things with the ranch."

"But I have a new assignment for you."

"That's nice," Creed said as he escorted Liza to the door.

"How long will you be gone?"

"I don't know."

"Don't make it too long. I—"

The door closed behind them.

Faraday looked at the others, who were grinning from ear to ear. He said, "Did I mention to him that the job was for a new railroad in Texas?"

A Look At: The Crocketts':
Western Saga One

SADDLE UP FOR A NON-STOP RIDE IN VOLUME ONE OF A NEW WESTERN SAGA – FROM THE MAN WHO BROUGHT YOU THE CHANEY BROTHERS WESTERN SERIES.

During the Civil War, they sought justice outside of the law, paying back every Yankee raid with one of their own. No man could stop them… no woman could resist them… and no Yankee stood a chance when Will and Gid Crockett rode into town.

After their parents are murdered by a band of marauding Yankees, Will and Gid Crockett join William Quantrill and his gang of bloodthirsty raiders to seek revenge on the attackers.

Someone's about to mess with the Crocketts', and that means someone's about to be messed with back. Will and Gid don't like getting shot at, especially by varmints who don't have skill enough to kill them.

The Crocketts': Western Saga 1 includes: Trail of Vengeance, Slaughter in Texas, Law of the Rope and The Town That Wouldn't Die.

AVAILABLE NOW ON KINDLE

About The Authors

Robert Vaughan sold his first book when he was 19. That was 57 years and nearly 500 books ago. His books have hit the NYT bestseller list seven times. He has won the Spur Award, the PORGIE Award (Best Paperback Original), the Western Fictioneers Lifetime Achievement Award, received the Readwest President's Award for Excellence in Western Fiction, is a member of the American Writers Hall of Fame and is a Pulitzer Prize nominee.

James Reasoner has been a professional writer for nearly forty years. In that time, he has authored several hundred novels and short stories in numerous genres. Writing under his own name and various pseudonyms, his novels have garnered praise from Publishers Weekly, Booklist, and the Los Angeles Times, as well as appearing on the New York Times, USA Today, and Publishers Weekly bestseller lists. He lives in a small town in Texas with his wife, award-winning fellow author Livia J. Washburn.